The Iron Road Home

by
Laurel Nebel

April 1 & 1999 Royal Fireworks Publishing
All Rights Reserved.

Royal Fireworks Press
First Avenue, P.O. Box
Unionville, NY 10988-0399
Tel: 738-8434
Fax: (914) 726-3824
email: rfpress@frontiernet.net

ISBN 0-880-464-2

Royal Fireworks Press
Unionville, New York

Royal Fireworks Press, Inc.
1 First Avenue, PO Box 399
Unionville, NY 10988-0399
(914) 726-4444
FAX: (914) 726-3824
email: rfpress@frontiernet.net

ISBN: 0-88092-466-7

Printed in the United States of America using vegetable-based inks on acid-free, recycled paper by the Royal Fireworks Printing Co. of Unionville, New York.

Acknowledgements

To my editor, Myrna Kemnitz: thank you for "seeing" my heart in this story and for wanting to publish it. And to Carol Lake, Pat Mauser, Peggy King Anderson and my sister, Marcia Corum, each of whom provided valuable editorial criticism and moral support throughout the manuscript process.

To all the hoboes I've met while researching this story, my sincere appreciation for your gentlemanly ways, and for welcoming me to your gatherings in Dunsmuir and Marquette.

Most especially to Guitar Whitey Symmonds, Choo Choo Johnson, and editor of the *Hobo Times*, Buzz Potter, my deep gratitude for your counsel, your friendship, and for sharing with me the lore of—and your long-enduring love for—the iron road.

And to my Blackwater Bobby, my husband Tom, who came late to the game but loved every mile of track, and who has Frankie and Blackie in his heart.

Thank you all for making my dream come true.

Dedication

To my favorite hobo in the whole world, Monte Holm of Moses Lake, Washington, who in the early 1930's rode the rails throughout the American west. True to the hobo creed, he has always shared what he has, little or much, and does so today—including his marvelous hobo stew.

Monte Holm, the "genuine article," a wonderful human being and my much loved friend.

1953: THE GREAT NORTHERN "HIGH LINE"

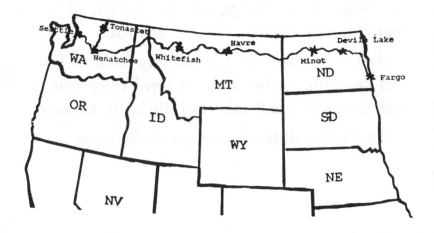

Devils Lake, North Dakota
January, 1953

Snow muffled the wheeze of an eastbound steam engine idling at the Devils Lake train station. Frankie Cooper and her mother wrestled cardboard suitcases along the path toward town. An icy wind tugged at their tattered coats. Frankie's hands and feet were freezing. After her mother had been fired this last time, there hadn't been enough money for gloves or boots.

Shivering, Frankie dropped her bags and stuffed her hands into her coat pockets. Frankie stamped her feet and peered up the deserted street. Devils Lake seemed small compared to Minot, N.D., the last town they had lived in. Maybe this one would be different. She hoped so.

After several moments, she blew on her hands, adjusted her threadbare scarf more securely around her neck and pulled her ragged cap down farther over her curly red hair. Sucking in a breath, she picked up the battered cases and trudged after her mother.

In the waning twilight, Mrs. Cooper stopped under a street lamp to peer at a slip of paper. She pointed toward a two-story building farther down the street and motioned Frankie to catch up.

Abruptly, Frankie stopped, the suitcases bumping against her legs. Green eyes wide with dismay, she stared at the seedy-looking wood structure. Above the building's listing front stoop, an old sign read:

ZIGFELT HOTEL
$2.50 WEEKLY

"Momma," she blurted out, "the conductor must've been wrong. We can't...live there. It's...."

She choked on the rest. Living in yet another rundown hotel was more than thirteen-year-old Frankie Cooper's mind wanted to accept.

Phone Here

Bad Area

Unsafe Area

Good Area

CHAPTER 1

Life at the Zigfelt

Frankie watched the Great Northern freight rumble toward the far end of the railyard. She blew a puff of air up through her tangled, sweaty bangs and shifted several books to her right arm. "Criminy, how'm I going to get across?" she grumbled. "If I'm not in the hotel pretty soon, Ziggy's going to have a fit." To her consternation, the steam locomotive with its line of freight cars rolled to a stop, blocking her way. Why hadn't she run faster?

Down the tracks, three hobos jumped from a boxcar, arguing. Bedrolls slung over shoulders, they headed toward a grove of trees behind several grain elevators. One of the men split off and disappeared. Seconds later, he reappeared on the other side heading for town. *Did he crawl underneath?* she wondered. *Must've.* The train was stopped. *Why not?* As she stepped toward a flatcar and crouched down, she felt a hand grip her shoulder.

"Don't even consider it, kid." The man's voice was as gentle as his grasp was firm, but his words were a definite command.

"But, that guy did." Frankie looked up into eyes as blue as the wind-washed Dakota sky overhead. The man in his early thirties was tall, muscular, in a faded red and blue plaid shirt, Levis, and an old sheepskin jacket, much like her own clothes. A sweat-stained gray hat covered black hair, his face unshaven. *Another hobo looking for work,* she guessed.

"He was lucky," the man said. Before he could continue, Frankie heard a clank and the freight jerked into motion.

Frankie flinched, realizing how close she'd come to getting hurt.

"See? I saw a fella lose a leg last fall."

"Oh," Frankie gulped. She stared at him wide-eyed, oblivious to the engine now shunting empty cars onto a siding next to the elevators.

"Don't do something stupid, kid. You're too pretty to get yourself killed."

"Yes, sir," Frankie stammered. "I won't." He nodded, hitched his bedroll higher on his back and headed down the tracks, his legs slightly bowed. Frankie yelled, "Thanks, mister!"

Still walking, the hobo turned and smiled. "You're welcome, kid. Remember what I said. Riding the rails is dangerous." He waved, and Frankie watched him until he disappeared behind the elevators.

For some reason, an empty feeling washed over her. She didn't know why, but she hoped to see him again, yet knew it was doubtful. Like most of the hobos she'd seen who came through Devils Lake, he'd camp near the yard, repair rails, or load wheat for several days to earn a little money, then drift on.

After the tracks cleared, Frankie crossed at a dead run, raced past the small train station and down an alley. She took the hotel's back stairs two at a time, then skidded through an open door into a musty, second-floor hallway. As she rushed along the corridor, a mouse darted into a crack in a baseboard.

She paused in front of her door, mulling over her chores. Clean bathroom and lobby. Wash glasses for Ziggy. Chop vegetables for Mrs. O'Reilly. Wash dishes. Do homework.

She turned the door handle and pushed. It didn't budge. She tried again. Nothing.

"I didn't lock it," Frankie muttered. "Momma...? Cripes, she beat me home. But she's supposed to be at work."

Frankie stared at the paint-chipped door. "Momma, open the door! C'mon, Momma." Nothing. Then she knew. *Damn,* she swore to herself, *she's at it again.* Scowling, Frankie pulled a hairpin out of her hair, straightened it, and got to work on the ancient keyhole.

This wasn't the first time Abigale Cooper had locked Frankie out. Her daughter had jimmied locks before. After a bit, the door clicked open, and Frankie stepped through the doorway.

She wasn't overly surprised by the mess. During the three months they had lived at the hotel, their room had always looked shabby. It had two lumpy beds, two wooden chairs, a rickety dresser, and a sagging card table, its drooping middle propped up by her mother's romance magazines on top of an apple box. A rusty faucet dripped in the wall-mounted sink. Next to the sink, an open-shelved cabinet housed odds and ends of food, utensils, a hot-plate, and a dented coffee pot.

A bottle of sour milk propped up the window, a breeze tugging at frayed curtains. A tangle of clothes, bought at rummage sales and missions, spilled from the dresser and a half-empty bottle of wine lay under it. And sprawled across the bed, snoring softly, Frankie's mother clutched an empty beer bottle.

Since leaving Pullman, Washington, in 1949, Abigaile had lost one waitress or fry-cook job after another. Before, when she had kept house for Mr. Milner, life had been pretty stable, but after he died, she began to drink heavily. Jobs came and went, and they'd move to another town and another school for Frankie.

"Cripes," Frankie hissed, "can't you ever keep your promise? You swore you'd stop!" Abigale mumbled something in her sleep. Frankie rolled her eyes. She knew her mother's promises were meaningless. Abigale always found a reason to start drinking again. An overly friendly boss. A boyfriend. Always something, whether she was happy or sad.

"Well, you won't need this." Frankie yanked the beer bottle out of her mother's hand and tossed it in the trash. Frankie covered her mother with a blanket and brushed a strand of blonde hair off Abigale's face. For a long moment, she looked at her mother. "I love you Momma, but sometimes you make me so angry. I wish you wouldn't drink." She sighed. "I hope you didn't get fired again, 'cause I'd like to stay here." She smiled sadly. "Maybe you'll find somebody nice. Yeah…and get married. Then we'd have a home. A real home." But Frankie knew her dreams of a home like other kids had, were just that—dreams.

In a whirlwind of frustrated energy, she dumped out the wine, straightened the room, and then hurried down the hall to clean the bathroom they shared with other lodgers and a family of mice.

"That you, Frankie?" Mr. Helman shouted as Frankie bounded down into the lobby. He sat at a wooden table with four elderly cronies assessing grimy cards, his eyes watery and squinting behind thick, wire-rimmed spectacles. Before Frankie could reply, he lifted bony, parchment-skin hands toward her to examine his cards. "What ya think, girl?"

Frankie peered over his shoulder. After a moment, she lifted her gaze to study the disheveled group for hints of their mood. When she had lived in Pullman, Mr. Milner had taught her how to play poker. The only one without a glum face was Mr. Wilbee, and he was a notorious bluffer. Wilbee boasted eighty-two years of hearty age, and the other four weren't far behind. What little hair Wilbee had was plastered around his smiling, cherubic face.

"Chester needs all the help he can get, Frankie." Wilbee chuckled and tossed another penny into the pot.

"Throw these away, Mr. Helman." Frankie touched the tops of two worn cards. "I think you'll get a couple better ones."

"Did ya get your story rewrit?" the old man queried, throwing the discards on the table.

"Yeah, Mrs. Holloway really likes it. She kept me after school today to check spelling and grammar. She thinks I might win a prize the newspaper is giving. But for a while she wasn't sure a girl knew how to play poker. At least no eighth grader."

"How'd ya convince her?"

"Showed her my journal. Didn't want to 'cause, well, you know. Other kids don't...." Frankie grimaced. "Never mind, I gotta get to work."

"Hope that teacher keeps quiet." Helman said, watching Frankie as she emptied ashtrays into a coffee-can spittoon. "Kid's got enough problems without her schoolmates knowin' she lives in this dump."

Built at the turn of the century and never maintained, the hotel had gone steadily down hill. In the lobby, a broken-down horsehair sofa leaned against dirty windows overlooking the street, and three decrepit armchairs sagged around a moth-eaten bear rug. The place reeked of unwashed bodies, stale cigarette smoke, and mice droppings.

"We all like the kid, Chester," Wilbee said, "but forget it. Ain't nothin' we can do. I got two fours and a coupla tens. Got anything better?"

"Yep," Helman said. With a toothless grin, he slapped three sixes onto the table and raked in a small pile of pennies. The game resumed, Frankie forgotten.

As she finished up her housekeeping, Frankie paused to glance at a *Life* magazine on the battered coffee table. It lay open to a photograph of President Eisenhower's grandchildren sitting on the White House steps. *Pretty kids,* she thought, smiling. *Wouldn't it be nice...? Forget it.* She flipped the magazine shut and with it, her dreams of having a "regular" family.

Ziggy, the balding, pot-bellied hotel owner, leaned against the counter in the bar. He was well past sixty and almost as wide as he was short. Yellow sweat rings stained the underarms of his frayed white shirt. As he pulled drafts of beer, he puffed on a foul-smelling cigar, a bluish fog drifting above his head.

"Where ya been, kid?" He pushed a slopping mug down the bar toward the closest of three ranch hands. "Need some clean mugs and glasses, pronto." He turned away when another man joined the group at the bar.

"Yes sir." Frankie darted behind the counter, relieved he hadn't chewed her out, and set to work. Drying the last mug, she yelled, "See you tomorrow," and hurried across the lobby to the cafe kitchen.

"Hello, dearie," chimed Mrs. O'Reilly, who ran the cafe. She was plump, her graying hair netted in a bun. Opening the oven door to remove two apple pies, she said, "Made a batch of oatmeal cookies. Get some milk, then start on the potatoes and carrots. Pot roast tonight."

After Frankie got the milk and a handful of cookies, Mrs. O'Reilly said, "Saw your mum. Isn't her job at the hospital working out?"

"Uh...sh-she must have a cold or something," Frankie lied. "Where's my apron?"

Mrs. O'Reilly raised an eyebrow questioningly. "On the peg where it always is, dear."

Frankie grabbed her apron and wrapped it around her skinny body. Between bites of cookie and gulps of milk, she peeled vegetables.

The hotel had a reputation for tasty meals and cheap drinks. The cafe was soon bustling. After the last customer left, Frankie and Mrs. O'Reilly sat down to plates heaped with mashed potatoes and gravy, beef, carrots and peas.

"Oh, that was so good!" Frankie wiped her plate clean with a chunk of bread.

"Not bad, if I say so myself," Mrs. O'Reilly said. "After dishes and homework, there's apple pie. Got any tests tomorrow?"

"Spelling test. That'll be easy. Some arithmetic and I gotta recite 'The Midnight Ride of Paul Revere.' But I've got that almost memorized."

The woman chuckled. "Well, give the pots a lick and a promise, 'cause I'd love to hear Paul Revere." From the first day, when Frankie had coaxed Eileen O'Reilly into letting her work in exchange for dinner, she'd been encouraged by the woman's interest in her studies. Often, when business was slow or chores done, Frankie would read to her.

Frankie polished the last skillet and settled down at a small table in the rear of the cafe to study. She worked through arithmetic, then hurried on to spelling. It was after ten before she got to the poem. She preferred mysteries and adventure stories but read everything she could get her hands on. When there was no lunch money, Frankie spent lunchtime reading in the school library to ward off hunger pangs.

A commotion in the lobby distracted her. The lobby fell silent for a moment until she heard a familiar, high-pitched wail.

"Where's my wine?" Abigale Cooper shrieked. "Frances Jane Cooper, whaddya do with my wine!"

Abigale used Frankie's birth name only when she was angry with her. Frankie hated "Frances" and had changed it. Her father's name had been Frank, and she figured if he were alive, he wouldn't mind.

Frankie bolted out of the cafe and into the lobby. On the second-floor landing, Abigale lurched in a drunken stupor toward the stairway.

"Wait!" Frankie yelled. "Don't, Momma!"

Abigale turned, waving the empty wine bottle at Frankie. "Where's my...?" She stumbled and fell against the banister. It creaked, swayed, and crashed to the lobby floor, Abigale with it.

CHAPTER 2

Alone

Frankie froze in mid-stride, staring at her mother's crumpled body. "Momma!" she cried.

Silence fell over the lobby, broken only by the rummaging of mice in the sofa. Horrified, Frankie fell to her knees beside her mother. Tears welled up, and she tasted blood when she bit her lip to keep from crying. She looked up into a ring of faces that reflected her own horror.

"Do something!" she gasped. No one moved. Trembling, she lifted her mother into her arms.

"It's okay, Momma. We'll get a doctor. Damn it!" she yelled. "Get Doc Schultz! Momma's hurt. Hurt bad!"

Pandemonium broke out then, everyone speaking at once.

Ziggy tried to pull her away from her mother, but Frankie refused to let go.

"Ziggy, take your grubby hands off that girl," Mrs. O'Reilly shouted, whopping him over the head with a cake spatula coated with frosting.

"D-damn!" he sputtered, covering his balding head with sausage-like hands.

Mrs. O'Reilly whopped him again. "Watch your language!"

10

The woman knelt beside Frankie, pulling Abigale's faded print dress down over her knees. "Frankie, we'll get Doc Schultz." She nodded toward one of the men. "Teddy, get the Doc." He headed for the door.

"Momma's going to be okay, isn't she?" Frankie asked. "She's gotta, Mrs. O'Reilly. She can't die." Heart pounding in her throat, she said shakily to her mother, "Let me tell you a story, Momma." And she began to recite "The Midnight Ride of Paul Revere."

"Listen, my children, and you shall hear
Of the midnight ride of Paul Revere.
On the eighteenth of April, in Seventy-five,
Hardly a man is now alive..."

Frankie choked on the last line. Tears bubbled over, spilling down her thin, freckled face. "You can't die, Momma," she wailed. "Please don't die."

Gently she rocked her mother until a gravelly man's voice barked, "Let me through." She looked up as a short, older man pushed his way through the onlookers, reading glasses cockeyed on his pepper-gray head. Dismay was evident in his eyes.

"Let me have a look-see, Frankie," he said softly, kneeling beside her and Abigale. Without looking up, he commanded. "I need some elbow room! Ziggy, get these folks out of here! Teddy, get my stretcher! And Eileen—make Frankie some cocoa."

With gentle hands, Doc Schultz lifted Frankie's tear-streaked face. "I'll do everything I can, Frankie. Now, go with Eileen while I see to your mother."

11

"But…."

"I'll do everything I can," he repeated. "Your medicine is a cup of cocoa. Up you go." He helped Frankie to her feet and handed her over to Mrs. O'Reilly.

Frankie heard bits of conversation as the last stragglers walked toward the bar.

"I'll bet you five," rasped a woman in a red dress, "she busted her fool neck."

"Hold your tongue, Milly!" a ranch hand shot back. "Her mom's all that kid's got. If Abigale's dead, then what? Kid don't got no other family." He spat a stream of tobacco at a coffee-can spittoon and missed. "Least none I hear tell of. It'll be the orphanage for Frankie, and I wouldn't wish that on my worst enemy."

Wide-eyed, Frankie watched the couple disappear into the bar. *No, no, no!* her mind screamed after them. *Momma isn't going to die! She can't.* Shaky and blinking back tears, she followed Mrs. O'Reilly into the cafe. "Doc will fix Momma up, won't he? She won't die, will she?"

"Don't know, darlin'," the woman replied bleakly, entering the kitchen. "If anyone can do anything for your mum, Doc Schultz can." She sounded doubtful.

"But she can't die."

"Sweetheart, all we can do is pray." Eyes downcast, Mrs. O'Reilly sighed and moved toward the stove.

Soon the aroma of chocolate filled the kitchen, and Mrs. O'Reilly handed Frankie a cup. Frankie numbly took it, sipping the brew absently as she watched the lobby. Teddy and a good looking, well-dressed man she didn't know lifted her mother onto the stretcher. The man's eyes settled on Frankie, and he said something to the doctor.

Doc Schultz nodded and walked toward Frankie in the cafe, his face pinched. It was the same look Frankie had seen on her mother's face when Mr. Milner had died.

"No!" she moaned, dropping the cup. "She can't be.... Momma can't die."

But the doctor's face told her Abigale was dead. Frankie's knees buckled, and the doctor caught her.

"Grab a chair, Eileen," he said. "We gotta get some air into her before she passes out."

Mrs. O'Reilly got the kitchen stool, and Doc Schultz sat Frankie on the edge, pushing her head between her knees. "Breathe," he said. "Breathe deep. That's it. Good. Again. Good girl."

After a couple of minutes, Frankie struggled to her feet. Mrs. O'Reilly wrapped her arms around the girl and Frankie leaned against her, crying. "Momma isn't really dead, is she?" she said hiccuping. She knew it was crazy to ask, but the reality of it all was too horrible. What would she do without her mother? She had hated Abigale's drinking, but her mother didn't deserve to die. Abigale was all Frankie had.

Eileen O'Reilly hugged Frankie closer, gazing up at the ceiling. Tears glistened in her own eyes.

The doctor sighed. "I'm sorry, Frankie. There wasn't anything I could do." Swiftly he changed subjects. "Eileen, take care of Frankie till I get things handled." His eyes shifted toward the lobby where Frankie could see her mother and the two men.

In a quavering voice, Frankie asked, "What are you gonna do with Momma?"

"Take her to the funeral home."

"Ohhh," she whimpered. Her gaze shifted from the doctor to the cook. She sucked in a shallow breath. "I wanna see Momma before you take...take her away."

"Oh my," Mrs. O'Reilly gulped. "Why don't you wait until tomorrow?" Frankie shook her head, swallowed hard and forced herself to walk into the lobby. The doctor and cook followed her.

"Oh, Momma," Frankie chocked, dropping down beside her mother's body. Hesitantly she picked up Abigale's hand. Frankie felt like her heart was being ripped out and she cried. Finally spent, she kissed her mother's cheek. "I'm...I'm gonna miss you, Momma, something awful." She sniffed and smiled sadly. "Now you and Daddy can be together like you always wanted."

Feeling drained and unable to think clearly, Frankie struggled to her feet and stumbled toward the stairs. "I don't feel very good. I'm going to bed."

"Don't think you can stay here alone, Frankie," Doc Schultz said, motioning the men to take Abigale away. "For now, you'd best come with me. I'll put you up for the night. I got a day bed in my office."

14

Mrs. O'Reilly frowned. "Doc, that won't work. I don't mean to interfere, but with you bein' a bachelor and all...."

"Dang," he grumbled, "you're right." He scratched his stubbled chin. "How about you puttin' her up for a few days till we figure out what the Sam Hill we're going to do?"

"Well," the cook said, "I could move Jocelyn in with Kathy and Elizabeth."

Frankie interrupted. "It's okay, Mrs. O'Reilly. I'll stay here. I appreciate it, but you already got seven kids. I'll be okay. I'll lock the door."

"Well, maybe," the woman said uneasily. "What do you think, Doc?"

The old man squinted at Frankie. "You got a chair in your room?" Frankie nodded. "Okay. Eileen and I'll agree to let you stay only if you shove the chair under the knob. Don't think anyone would bother you, but it's best to be on the safe side. Now, where are your folks, Frankie?"

"Folks?"

"Your dad. Grandparents, aunts, uncles."

She looked at him blankly. "There was just Momma. My dad died before I was born." She sniffed and wiped her eyes with the back of her hand.

Flustered, the doctor muttered, "But surely your mom's got folks. A mother, father, brothers, sisters?"

"Probably," Frankie answered, "but Momma never talked about them."

Under his breath he swore, then puffed out his cheeks in exasperation. "Well, what about your dad's folks? You must've met them."

"Un-uh. At least, I don't remember them."

"Sweet Jesus," he sputtered.

Frankie looked at him defiantly. "It's not that I didn't ask. Momma just wouldn't talk about them."

It hadn't seemed strange to Frankie that her mother didn't talk about her family at the time. It was just the way things were. But now, she couldn't help wondering why.

"It was like she was mad at them or something. Sometimes, though," she said slowly, remembering, "when she'd been drinking, Momma talked about Dad. He got killed in the war."

She paused, looking at them glumly. "That was when I was little and we lived with Mr. Milner. Sometimes I'd sneak downstairs for a cookie and some milk after I'd been sent to bed. One time I hear Momma talking about Dad. She loved him a lot."

A fleeting smile crossed her face. "Momma said I look like him, red hair, freckles, green eyes...." Her mind leapfrogged back to the conversation in the lobby. She blurted, "You won't send me to an orphanage, will you?"

Mrs. O'Reilly grimaced. "Oh my goodness, no. Not if we can help it." She didn't look overly certain, and neither did the doctor.

Apprehensive, Frankie glanced from one to the other. Somehow, she had to convince them she should stay at the hotel. Her mind whirled. Before either of them could say anything, she plunged ahead. "I bet I could talk Ziggy into letting me stay here, since we swapped cleaning for our room. And if I can still work for you, Mrs. O'Reilly, all I'll need are some odd jobs for clothes and stuff." She paused, waiting for a response. The doctor and cook looked dumbfounded. She hurried on. "Oh, c'mon. It'd work, wouldn't it?"

Doc Schultz shrugged, his face troubled. "I don't know, Frankie."

Frankie could almost see thoughts whirring around in his head. He looked dubious. "Ziggy's got a major problem with your mother's accident. If it was just between me and the sheriff, I think I could pressure Ziggy into letting you stay, but the county's another matter. Now, if you were older, fifteen or sixteen, the authorities might look the other way." He sighed. "I'll try to work something out."

"Thanks," Frankie said, exhaustion washing through her. "I'm goin' t' bed. I'm tired. Real tired." She started up the steps, Doc Schultz on her heels.

Eileen O'Reilly caught his sleeve. "Let her go, Doc. She'll be better in the morning."

The cook called after her, "Frankie, remember the chair."

Frankie nodded and trudged on, her mind numb with grief.

In a daze, Frankie let herself into the room. She locked the door and pushed a chair under the knob. Without undressing, she crawled into bed. "Momma, Momma," she sobbed into her pillow. "What am I going to do?"

Dead End

No One Home

Unfriendly Town

Camping

Good Water

CHAPTER 3

A Fight

"Momma!" Frankie yelped. She jerked upright in bed, drenched in sweat.

Trembling, she slid under the covers again, the nightmare still vivid in her mind—a dream of grabbing her mother's hand and Abigale slipping away and falling, falling, falling into darkness.

The horror of the previous hours slammed into Frankie like a runaway train. What-ifs whirled around in her head. *What if I hadn't poured the wine down the drain? What if the banister hadn't broke? Momma might be alive if only she hadn't gotten drunk....* She cried herself back to sleep.

Eyes red and puffy, Frankie woke to the sound of muffled voices in the hall the next morning. It was past eight o'clock, and she knew she'd be late for school. Like a sleepwalker, she changed clothes, ate some stale crackers and peanut butter, and shuffled off to school. The notion that she didn't have to go never crossed her mind.

Mrs. Holloway looked up as Frankie slipped through the door and tiptoed to her desk. Paul Pritchard, a sandy-haired boy, watched her, turned and whispered something to another boy nearest him. The teacher called for silence and the geography lesson resumed.

When the recess bell rang, Frankie debated whether to tell Mrs. Holloway about her mother. *I better,* she thought, *'cause she'll find out anyhow.* But, before she could, the woman hurried out of the classroom with a handful of papers.

Uncertain about what to do next, Frankie went outside. At the bottom of the backyard steps, she heard Paul Pritchard talking.

"Yeah! She broke her stupid neck," he said in a know-it-all tone. "Teddy tol' me she was drunk as a skunk and fell over the banister." The cluster of kids was so taken with Paul's tale they didn't notice Frankie join them.

She stood at the rear of the group and listened. *Momma. They're talking about Momma.* Frankie swallowed hard and blinked back tears, wondering who Teddy was. Then she remembered. *Teddy had fetched Doc Shultz's stretcher.*

"And my brother said she was drinkin' at the Railhead Tavern with some guys," Paul continued.

Frankie turned to leave. *Why do they have to talk about Momma that way?* she wondered. She hated being reminded of her mother's drinking and how, from time to time, some man would bring Abigale home after a binge.

Before Frankie could sneak away, the boy said something which made her feel like she'd been punched in the stomach.

"And you know what else? Frankie lives in the Zigfelt Hotel!" The other children pressed closer, clamoring for more. He laughed. "Yeah, no wonder she looks like a bum. She lives with 'em!" Gales of laughter erupted.

Anger surged through Frankie. *A bum!* she seethed. Kids often made fun of her clothes, but this was enough. She shoved kids aside to reach Paul.

"Oh yeah?" she snarled.

"Yeah," he taunted, pushing her to the ground. She scrambled to her feet and lunged for him. By the time the principal and a teacher pulled them apart, Paul had a bloody nose and Frankie had a swollen eye.

After marching them to her office and tending to their injuries, the principal admonished them for fighting.

"And Paul, I am disappointed in you," Mrs. Gibson finished. "How could you be so mean?!" To Frankie she said more gently, "Why don't you go home until after the funeral, Frankie. I'm sorry about your mother." She ushered them both out into the hallway and closed the door. Paul shot off down the hall and disappeared around a corner.

Frankie stood for a moment in the empty corridor. She didn't care what Mrs. Gibson said. Paul deserved what he got, and she was proud of defending herself. Slipping out a side door, she headed for the hotel.

In the lobby she was cornered by a gray-haired, scrawny-necked woman with reading glasses perched on the tip of her long, thin nose. "The county has assigned me to your case," she said. "I'm supposed to find you a home." She blinked, staring at Frankie's injured eye.

"My God, you've been fighting." She peered reproachfully over the rim of her glasses. "No one will want to adopt a girl who fights!" More to herself than anyone else, she muttered, "Don't you ever comb your hair?" Frankie's red curls stuck out every which way with bits of grass and dirt clearly visible. "And your clothes!"

Frankie's face flushed. "You'd've punched Paul Pritchard, too, if he said you looked like a bum. So what if I buy clothes at the Sally? It's all we can afford." She sucked in a breath. "'Sides, lady, I already have a place to live. Doc Schultz said I could stay here."

"My word!" the woman sputtered, her cheeks suddenly splotches of pink.

While they were talking, a handful of lobby regulars had gathered around them.

"Tha's right, ma'am," Mr. Wilbee interrupted. "Ziggy told me this morning Frankie can stay as long as she likes." He grinned. "And if that don't work out," he added, nudging his friend, Helman, "me and Chester here'll adopt her." Helman nodded.

The woman's mouth dropped open. "What!" she squawked. "Are you crazy? There's no way men your age can adopt her." With a harrumph, she turned on her heel and stomped off toward the bar. "Ziggy knows better than to think that child can live here. After all, there are laws."

Helman peered at Frankie's eye. "Must've been quite a fight. What happened?"

Quickly, she explained. "I probably shouldn't have hit Paul, but he made me so mad." She smirked. "Bet he won't make fun of me again." The old men grinned and nodded.

Suddenly, Ziggy and the welfare worker burst from the bar, arguing.

"There's no reason Frankie can't stay here," Ziggy said hotly. "Who says she has to go to the children's home, anyway?"

"I do!" The woman's voice was adamant. "As long as I have a say in the matter, Frances Cooper will not reside in this dump!" Frankie stifled a laugh. The woman's remark hit home. Ziggy's jowly face turned beet red.

"Dump?" he snarled. "Frankie and her mom never complained about it! And let me tell you somethin' else, woman, Frankie can live here as long as she wants!" He paused a moment and chuckled. "And I 'magine District Supervisor Hartman just might agree with me. I do think a call's in order."

"You wouldn't call that despicable man!" The woman blanched. "Oh, I didn't mean to say that. He's.... Oh my goodness." Clutching her handbag to her flat chest, she bolted out of the hotel.

"Interestin'." Ziggy grinned at Frankie. "She don't like her boss, Hartman, any better than I hear he likes her. That should keep her off our backs for a few days.

23

You can stay as long as you like, kid. A deal's a deal."
Then he sobered. "I don't know if I can pull it off,
but I'll try."

"Oh, you better get on over to the funeral home.
Mrs. O'Reilly's over there with the Doc, makin'
arrangements. Sorry about your mom, Frankie."

Before lumbering off to the bar, he chortled.
"You're gonna have one humdinger of a shiner come
mornin'. Hope you walloped 'im good."

"Thanks for letting me stay," she called after him.
She turned to Helman and Wilbee. "And thank you two
for wanting to adopt me."

Frankie didn't know whether to laugh or cry. Two
lovable old codgers wanted to adopt her but couldn't,
and the likelihood of her being sent to an orphanage
was real. And there was her fight with Paul, and now
Momma's funeral to think about.

Blinking back tears, she said softly, "I guess I better
go."

"Want us to go with you?" Helman asked. He, too,
looked like he might cry.

"It's okay, Mr. Helman," she said, patting his bony
shoulder. She swallowed the lump in her throat and
hurried outside.

On the outskirts of town, Frankie found the Spalding
Funeral Home. The mortuary was an impressive,
two-story gabled wood building surrounded by flower
gardens and maple trees. Slowly, she climbed the stone
front steps.

Heavy-hearted, she commanded herself to open the door. Seeing her mother wasn't something she wanted to do. It made it all so final. But she knew she must. Once inside, she looked around but saw no one in either the foyer or the long hallway.

Beyond a small empty chapel, she heard Mrs. O'Reilly shout, "Charles Spalding, how can you be so heartless! The woman deserves a decent burial."

"What's the matter?" Frankie asked, forgetting how upset she felt, and entered a beautifully furnished office. Seated behind a mahogany desk was the handsome man Frankie had seen the night before. His musky aftershave hung in the air. Frankie's nose wrinkled involuntarily. *Phew,* she thought. *How can he wear that stuff?*

"Slight disagreement, is all," Doc Schultz said, seated with Mrs. O'Reilly opposite the mortician. "Nothing we can't iron out." The doctor's face was flushed, and Frankie could tell he was as angry as Eileen O'Reilly. "Isn't that right, Charlie?" he added hotly.

Spalding shrugged. "I assume this young lady is Mrs. Cooper's daughter?"

Frankie nodded.

For a moment Spalding studied her. Something in his gaze was unsettling, but Frankie dismissed her unease as being nervous about the funeral.

"Ziggy will cover the funeral, but he doesn't have enough money for a tombstone. I won't bury your mother without some kind of marker."

"What!" Frankie sputtered, eyes flashing. "What are you going to do? Plant her in the garden with your flowers?" She knew she was being flippant, but what was this man thinking of?

He laughed, seeming to enjoy her spunk. "Sort of. We have an area for poor folk. But if you come up with the money for a marker, she'll get a proper burial."

Frankie struggled to control her temper. *All he cares about is money,* she thought. In addition to the office, she could see it provided him with a well-tailored suit, gold tie tack and cuff links—all signs of a profitable business.

Money. I need money. Where can I get it? She scanned the room. Then she found the solution.

"You have a nice place, sir, but whoever cleans it doesn't do a very good job." She moved over to his desk and ran a finger around the base of his brass desk lamp. She forced a smile.

"Dust. I swap cleaning for Momma's and my room at Ziggy's hotel. If you bury Momma proper, with a tombstone and all, I'll work here every Saturday and Sunday till her bill's paid."

Charles Spalding ran long fingers through his dark, silver-tipped hair and rose to his feet. "Hmm. You're an interesting one. Not only pretty but industrious, too."

He gave her a slow, easy smile. "I admire you for wanting to see your mother buried properly." He straightened the knot in his striped tie and stood up.

"But there is more to the job than mere cleaning, if you know what I mean."

Frankie didn't.

"Don't suppose you'd want to help me prepare bodies for burial?"

Frankie shuddered and shook her head.

"Didn't think so." He rocked back and forth on his heels, stroking his chin. "Tell you what I'll do, though. Eventually, Ziggy will have to give you up to the authorities. No reason for you to worry about the orphanage, though. The hired girl my wife has doesn't seem to be working out and, by coincidence, will be leaving in a couple of days. Ziggy says you're a good worker, and I'm sure my wife would find you a big help."

"Really!" Frankie exclaimed. "You'll let me work it off?"

But for some reason she felt uneasy. *Ziggy? Why would he talk to Ziggy,* she wondered. *Strange.* Even so, she knew she didn't have any other choice. It was either work for Spalding, or her mother would end up in an unmarked grave like the bums and winos. Paul Pritchard would taunt her for sure. *No way. Momma wasn't a bum.* And besides, she didn't want to go to an orphanage.

Shut Up

Anything Goes

27

CHAPTER 4

Letters

"The Sally can always use more clothes," Mrs. O'Reilly had said, giving Frankie some twine to bundle Abigale's clothes for the Salvation Army.

Eileen O'Reilly and Ziggy had kept her busy morning to night these past three days, cleaning and doing her regular chores. Frankie knew why. She hadn't had time to brood about her mother and was grateful. Earlier, she'd stripped Abigale's and her beds and cleaned their room. Behind her mother's iron bedstead, stuffed against the wall, she'd found the satchel—Abigale's "treasure," guarded even from Frankie. From time to time, in one town or another, Frankie had wakened at night to see her mother sitting at a table, smoking, drinking coffee, and reading papers from it.

After taking the bundle to the Sally, Frankie sat cross-legged on the floor in soft morning sunshine, the shabby curtains above her rustling in the April breeze. She emptied the satchel on the floor. A jumble of papers and a hard-bound Rudyard Kipling novel fell out. She opened the book and saw an inscription:

February 11, 1922

Happy Birthday, son,
Now you have your very own copy. Hope
you enjoy Kim as much as I have.

Love, Mom

There was also a letter addressed to Frankie's mother tucked inside the book. She unfolded it and began to read.

July 16, 1939

Dearest Abigale,

Keep this safe until I get back. Hopefully,
it won't be long until we bomb the hell out of
the Nazis. Then we'll get sent home and you and
I can sit in the orchard again and read.

I know how much you love being read to, so
I'll leave this in your care until I return. When
I wasn't pestering Mr. Pratt to fly, I was reading. I
have a copy I'll take to England.

I'd rather be home with you, but the RCAF
will let me fly all I want. Besides, the USA
will be in it before long, and I'd have to go
anyway.

Loving you with all my heart,
Frank

"Ohhh," Frankie murmured, rereading the letter. She was soothed by her father's lovingness. Suddenly anger and frustration hit her full force. This was the first glimpse Frankie ever had of her father. Why hadn't Momma shared him with her?

She'd learned early on not to question Abigale about him. On the few occasions when she had, Abigale had become withdrawn and refused to talk. Other than her father's name, that he'd died during World War II and that she resembled him, Frankie knew nothing.

Occasionally, after Frankie had gone to bed, she'd heard her mother cry herself to sleep. Even Mr. Milner, the retired wheat rancher in Pullman where they'd been living at the time, skirted the topic, feigning ignorance.

The knowledge her father liked to read brought a smile to Frankie's lips. Maybe it explained her love of reading and why Abigale liked Frankie to read to her. But it didn't explain why her mother had refused to talk about him.

Is there anything else? Frankie wondered. She leafed through the pages of the book and found two news clippings. The first reported that Sergeant Pilot Frank Cooper had been shipped stateside after being wounded in England.

The next leaped at her:

LOCAL BOY DIES OF WOUNDS SUFFERED AFTER PLANE SHOT DOWN

There was a photograph of a bomber, Frankie's father, and his crew. The article told how Cooper managed to limp the plane in after losing part of a wing and an engine. He had crash-landed in a wheat field.

Later, his crew said Cooper had been determined they wouldn't be captured by the Germans. The article went on to tell of his love of flying and how Elmer Pratt, a local cattle rancher and orchardist, had taught him how to fly. For his bravery, Cooper had received several medals before being shipped home, only to die from complications. The article listed his surviving relatives. Parents: John and Patricia Cooper; Sisters: Rosemary and Anne; Brothers: James, William and Gordon, all of Tonasket, Washington. Cooper's burial mass was said on March 6, 1940, at the Tonasket Holy Rosary Catholic Church.

Frankie frowned. *Something isn't right.* She scanned the list of names. *Why wasn't Mama mentioned? After all, Abigale was his wife.*

Perplexed, she shook the book, looking for something that might offer an explanation. Only a cluster of dried blossoms drifted to the floor. Sure she'd missed something, she peered inside the bag and pried at the bottom. *No false bottom.* She ran her hand around the inside—something she'd read about in a book.

"Ah," she mused, feeling something behind the lining. With closer inspection, she found an open seam near the clasp. She pulled out a thin bundle of envelopes and photographs. She was elated at the discovery. Slowly, she studied each picture. One showed her mother and father in an orchard in full bloom. Frankie studied her parents' smiling faces. *Mmm,* she thought, *they really loved each other.* The next was a photo of her father in his Royal Canadian Air Force uniform.

Frankie had never thought of herself as being attractive, but her dad had been, and she smiled at the thought. If she cut her hair, she'd look like a younger version of the man in the photograph.

The last two pictures were of Frank Cooper with what must have been his family: his parents, three brothers and two sisters. Frankie sat mesmerized. For her whole life, Frankie had only her mother. But really, she had a grandfather and grandmother, and aunts and uncles! Strange there weren't photos of her mother's family. For the time being, she wouldn't worry about it. Could she find the Coopers? Somehow she would. She couldn't imagine how, but somehow, when she'd paid off her mother's marker, she'd find them.

The clipping said Dad was from Tonasket. Where in Washington is that? Do the Coopers still live there? All I gotta do is find Tonasket and ask around, she thought. She chewed on the inside of her lip. *But what if they don't believe I'm their granddaughter? Nah, they'll have to. I look like Dad and, with his stuff, they'll know I'm not lying.*

But how could she find them? A bus or train would cost a lot of money, which she didn't have. Without money, finding her grandparents would be impossible. Maybe she'd have time for some odd jobs while she worked off her mother's debt. She'd figure it out later.

Comforted by the photographs, she proceeded to read through the letters tied with a red ribbon. All were testaments of the love her father had felt for her mother. Again, she was assailed by mixed emotions—delight at finding her father's letters, and anger at her mother for not telling her more about him.

The fifth and final letter left her baffled.

August 23, 1939

Dearest Abigale,

*I've talked to my commanding officer, and there's
no way they can get me home and back in
time to ship out with the rest of my unit. But
when I get home, we'll do it up right. I promise.
There isn't anything more I'd rather do.*

*If your mother won't let you go home, go
to my parents. They'll understand.*

*If we have a little boy, I'd like him named
after my Dad. Maybe Frances Jane for a girl.
But, whatever you decide is fine with me.*

*Remember, if your mother won't let you go
home, Mom and Dad will take care of you until
I get back. But if worse comes to worse, Father
Joseph will help.*

*Hope the baby won't have my curly red hair.
Doesn't really matter, I suppose, just so it
has all his or her fingers and toes.*

With all my love,
Frank

*Do what up right? Father Joseph? Why had
Momma gone to Mr. Milner's rather than to her mother's
or to Dad's parents?*

Frankie felt confused beyond measure, but didn't have time to figure it out. She had to pack her own stuff and find a dress to wear to the funeral. She'd outgrown her one and only dress. As she jammed everything back into the satchel, she didn't notice the tip of another sheet of paper still tucked behind the lining.

Lugging her suitcase and the satchel, Frankie went downstairs. En route, she decided to keep her discovery to herself.

As she cut across the lobby toward the cafe, Ziggy lumbered out of the bar carrying a soup can, followed by Helman and Wilbee. The tin can jingled with each step.

"Sorry I can't make it to you mom's funeral, Frankie," Ziggy said. "Cliff was supposed to take over for me, but he got drunk last night and landed in jail."

He pushed the can toward her. "Wish there was more, but this is all we got. Hope it helps."

"Thank you," she said, peering into the can. It was half-full of change with several one and two-dollar bills. She smiled appreciatively at the men. "I'll save it for..." *Oops*, she thought, finishing with, "college." Maybe later she would tell them about her plan to find her grandparents. For now she would keep it to herself. Before they could comment, she changed subjects and tucked the can inside the satchel. "I gotta get to work."

The cafe hummed with activity. Frankie pitched in, making sandwiches and bussing tables while the cook encouraged customers to eat quickly.

"We got a funeral to attend," Mrs. O'Reilly said grimacing. She pointed to a cream pitcher next to the cash register. "Any tips or donations go in there to help Frankie pay for her mom's tombstone." To her surprise, Frankie saw the pitcher was nearly full. More money for her trip home. Certainly not enough, but it wouldn't be long.

As Mrs. O'Reilly removed plates from the counter, Frankie asked, "Does Elizabeth have a dress I can borrow? My old blue one's too small."

The woman paused and pursed her lips. "Only if I let down the hem, darlin'. And we don't have time." She cocked her head as she surveyed Frankie's attire. "Heavens alive, child, you need everything! Shoes, socks, pants, blouses. I hope Charlie Spalding springs for some new clothes. But from what I hear, it's his wife who controls the purse strings."

She forced a smile. "What do you think of Mrs. Spalding, Frankie?"

Frankie shrugged. "I don't know. I haven't met her."

"You haven't?"

"Un-uh. I asked Mr. Spalding about her at Momma's viewing, but he said she'd been out of town."

A frown furrowed Mrs. O'Reilly's brow. "Gone to Fargo, most likely. Can't understand why that old biddy married Charlie in the first place. Other than his good looks, he ain't much. And she's old enough to be his mother."

She studied Frankie for a moment. "Wish you hadn't talked yourself into working for him. Between the Doc and me, we'd have worked something out." She harrumphed. "Never liked Charlie from the start. Still can't figure why he's so all fired up to help you."

Frankie smiled half-heartedly, reluctant to admit she wondered the same thing. "It's okay, Mrs. O'Reilly, I couldn't let him bury Momma in the field behind the graveyard like the bums. Besides, it won't be long till the marker's paid off."

"Even so, he's a shifty character. You watch him, you hear? And let me know if he does anything he shouldn't."

The cook sighed, peering at the wall clock. "We're going to be late if I don't get these folks out of here."

She announced to the few stragglers that the cafe was about to close, and they needed to hurry. She fished some change out of the cream pitcher and handed it to Frankie. "Stop at the Sally and see if you can find something pretty to wear. I'll meet you at the church as soon as I close up."

Frankie slipped out the back door and hurried along the alley. As she rounded the corner, she stopped abruptly. Parked in front of the drugstore across the street was a blue Cadillac.

Charles Spalding was leaning into the driver's window arguing with the silver-gray-haired woman inside. Suddenly, the car door jutted open and a well-dressed woman stepped out. Frankie darted behind a parked pickup and watched.

"What do you mean, Jeanie left?" the woman said loudly.

Frankie couldn't hear Spalding's reply, but she could tell the woman wasn't happy with his answer.

"This is the third girl we've lost since we moved here. When Earl was alive, I never had trouble keeping a hired girl."

Spalding murmured something, and Frankie saw the woman frown. "Stole your watch? Not the one I gave you for Christmas?" Spalding nodded.

"Well, guess I'll just have to buy another one."

Again, Frankie couldn't hear Spalding's reply.

"My God, Charles, how will a thirteen-year-old ever manage to do all the cleaning, cooking, and still do her homework?"

Spalding put an arm around the woman. Frankie strained to hear what he said, but couldn't. After a moment, his wife pulled away from him.

"Well, if she doesn't work out, I won't let her stay, orphan or no orphan. Understood?"

Frankie watched as the woman entered the drug store, and Spalding got into a shinny blue Packard farther down the street. *Oh boy,* she thought, shaking her head. *What have I got myself into now?*

Judge's House

No Good   **Wealthy Folk**

Law Building

CHAPTER 5

A New Job

The last clods of dirt slipped through her fingers onto the casket. Face wet with tears, Frankie whispered, "I love you, Momma. I'm gonna miss you somethin' awful."

Out of the corner of her eye, she saw Spalding watching her. For reasons she didn't understand, the hairs on the back of her neck prickled. *Why's he watching me?* she wondered.

She cast a sideways glance at Doc Schultz and Mrs. O'Reilly to see if they'd noticed, but their eyes were downcast as though in prayer. Off to one side, Helman and Wilbee stood quietly talking to a few of their cronies. If they'd noticed, they didn't seem concerned.

Frankie dismissed her uneasiness as the product of an overactive imagination when Mrs. O'Reilly took her hand. "C'mon, darlin'," the woman said softly, "Ziggy's springin' for refreshments back at the hotel."

As Frankie followed the small group out of the cemetery, she gave a fleeting look at her mother's grave. *Momma, why'd you have to die?* she cried silently. Despair washed over her. The realization that her mother was gone and that she would never see her again assailed her. As quickly as the thought appeared, it vanished. Suddenly she was scared. *What am I going to do? What if I can't please Mrs. Spalding?* She wasn't sure if she could, but she'd have to try.

The rest of the afternoon passed in a haze of condolences and good-byes. By the time she'd hugged Doc Schultz, Ziggy, Helman, and Wilbee, she was ready to cry. She was going to miss the hotel a lot. The final good-bye would be the worst. Glumly she entered the cafe's kitchen.

"That you, dearie?" Mrs. O'Reilly called out, pouring cornbread batter into a pan. "Cookies baking, should be...." She stopped and looked up, shaking her head.

"Sorry, darlin'. It's going to be hard getting used to you not being here." Large tears glistened in the woman's eyes. One escaped and she wiped it away with the back of her hand. Frankie bit her lip to keep back tears. She didn't succeed.

"It's not like we won't see each other," the cook said, gathering Frankie in her arms.

After a couple of minutes, Frankie pulled away, rubbed her eyes and smiled half-heartedly. "I'll be okay. I just wish I could stay here, but I know I can't."

She took a deep breath and squared her shoulders. "Well, I better get going. I've got a feeling Mrs. Spalding isn't going to be easy to work for."

"Now, why'd ya say that?" Mrs. O'Reilly asked with a frown.

Frankie didn't want to upset her. "After you sent me to the Sally, I saw Mr. Spalding talking to his wife. I got the feeling she wasn't real happy about me working for them."

The cook's frown deepened. "Gossip has it Helen Spalding is demanding and hard to work for. Girls don't seem to stay long, I do know that. I just wish Patrick and I had a bigger house. Then you could live with us."

"It's okay, Mrs. O'Reilly," Frankie murmured, comforted that the woman cared. "I'll work it out. Maybe Mrs. Spalding's not as bad as people say." To herself she thought, *Boy, I hope so.*

She looked at the wall clock over the doorway, a reminder that she had to leave. "I gotta get over there, or Mrs. Spalding will yell at me for sure."

"Doc Schultz'll drop you off."

She shook her head. "It's okay. It isn't very far."

Before Mrs. O'Reilly could object, Frankie picked up her baggage and was out the back door on her way to the funeral home.

Passing the Sally, Frankie saw a group of hobos waiting for dinner. In the distance she heard the mournful cry of a Great Northern whistle. The sound reminded her of the blue-eyed hobo, and she looked for him. He wasn't around, which made her feel a little sad. He'd been nice, and he'd saved her from getting injured. *Had my father been like him, gentle and caring?* She smiled at the thought. *Probably.*

It was approaching five o'clock when she dropped her bags on the sidewalk in front of the funeral home. She wondered where the Spaldings lived. *Probably around back,* she concluded. She picked up her bags and walked to the rear of the building.

The grounds were impressive, skirted by maple trees and manicured lawns, with flower beds, and a four-car detached garage. Frankie saw Mrs. Spalding's blue Cadillac parked beside a gabled Victorian house. Charles Spalding's car was nowhere in sight.

Servants use the back door, Frankie reminded herself.

She puffed out her cheeks and exhaled, willing courage, then she clambered up the back steps onto the porch. She set her bags down, knocked on the door, and waited.

Nothing happened.

She tried again.

Again, nothing.

Wasn't she expected? She had to be. Hadn't she heard Spalding talking to his wife outside the drugstore? She stared at the blue-gray door, trying to decide what to do.

Maybe Mrs. Spalding is hard of hearing? Sure. That would explain it. As she turned the door knob and leaned forward, calling out, "Is anyone home?" the door jerked open and she fell to her knees.

"What do you think you're doing?" a shrill voice demanded. Looking up, Frankie saw Helen Spalding standing over her. She reeked of alcohol.

Startled and embarrassed, Frankie scrambled to her feet. "I'm sorry, ma'am," she stammered. "I did knock, but when...I...er...." Her face grew hot.

"Well?" the woman demanded haughtily, cutting her off.

Had Mrs. Spalding forgotten she was coming? Frankie searched for the right words to explain. "Mr. Spalding said I could work for you to pay off my mother's marker. She died and...I...I worked at the hotel, and...."

"So, you're Jeanie's replacement?" the woman interrupted. Her gray eyes narrowed with distaste at the sight of Frankie's black eye and old clothes.

"Well, it's about time you got here!" she snapped. "Cocktails are at seven. Dinner at eight. You'll find everything you need in the kitchen. Swiss steak tonight."

Swiss steak? That shouldn't be too hard, Frankie thought. She'd seen Mrs. O'Reilly prepare it. All she needed was a recipe.

"Menus for the next week are on the counter. Positively no substitutions," Mrs. Spalding said. "There's a list of your other duties as well. Breakfast is to be served at seven, lunch at twelve noon when you're not in school. You'll eat in the kitchen, of course."

Of course, Frankie thought, *where else do servants eat? With the pigs?* She bit the inside of her lip to keep quiet and just nodded politely.

"I expect fresh baked bread on Wednesdays and Saturdays. Tomorrow's Saturday!" With a long, red-painted fingernail, Mrs. Spalding flicked a piece of lint off Frankie's shirt sleeve.

Frankie stared at her wide-eyed. This once-beautiful woman, bedecked in a blue silk dress, pearl necklace and earrings, was going to be impossible to please. She stifled a shiver.

Mrs. Spalding peered at Frankie reproachfully. "How you dress for school is your business, but when you're here, you will always be in uniform. Understood?"

Flicking her nail again, she pointed down a hallway toward a stairway. "Your room is on the third floor. You'll find a uniform in the wardrobe."

"Yes, ma'am." Frankie stared after the woman who turned on her heel and disappeared through a doorway into what Frankie assumed was a living room—a room she was sure she was restricted from except when she was cleaning. *Hey, I can't help it that I couldn't find anything nice at the Sally,* she thought angrily.

She puffed out her cheeks in exasperation and headed outside to retrieve her bags. The woman was going to be a witch to work for, much like the social worker. With a sinking feeling, she remembered the bread she was supposed to make, not to mention the Swiss steak. Those were chores Mrs. O'Reilly had always handled herself. How was she ever going to manage? Well, she'd have to do what she could and hope for the best.

Her room in the attic had barely enough room for a bed, wardrobe, dresser, night stand, chair, and a lamp. The only appealing aspect were the two open windows letting in the late afternoon sun and air.

She put on the uniform. The last girl to wear it had been shorter and heavier than Frankie. "I'll have to let down the hem and take in some seams," she said to herself, wrapping the ties of the stiff white apron around her waist twice.

Peering at herself in the mirror, she wanted to laugh. She looked ridiculous in the ill-fitting black skirt and over-sized white blouse. She looked no more like a maid than the man in the moon. But she couldn't worry about it, she had a deadline to keep. She bounded out of the room and down the stairs to the kitchen.

In a gut-wrenching frenzy, Frankie found an extensive set of cookbooks. Relieved, she quickly saw the Swiss steak wouldn't be hard to prepare. She started dinner, read how to make martinis, and served the meal and drinks only three minutes late.

After dinner, sipping her fourth glass of wine, Mrs. Spalding said to her husband, "Before the Andersens come next Saturday, the girl will need proper shoes." She lifted an eyebrow and looked at Frankie. "And that mop of red hair has to go."

Charles Spalding leaned back in his chair, giving Frankie the once-over. He smiled at his wife. "So she passed the test, I take it?"

45

"For the time being," Mrs. Spalding replied indifferently.

With a wink only Frankie saw, Spalding rose. "Dinner was good, Frankie, and I'm sure Mrs. Spalding will overlook the delay this time."

Smiling broadly at his wife, he continued, "Helen, you're right about Frankie's hair. But wouldn't ribbons be cheaper than a haircut?"

He stood and motioned Frankie over. He pulled her hair away from her face into a loose pony tail. "Like this, darling."

Frankie stiffened and stepped backward, feeling uneasy, hair falling past her shoulders. *What is it with this guy?* she wondered.

Spalding continued undaunted, "A black ribbon tied in a bow would look nice. I'll be in Fargo Monday and I'll pick some up then."

Helen Spalding slowly got to her feet. As she caught the edge of the table to keep from falling, she knocked over her wine glass. Blood red wine splashed across the white table cloth. Frankie cringed, wondering how she'd get the stain out. "Just as long as she makes a good impression," she said, slurring her words and turning to her husband. "I could use a brandy, Charles. Shall we?"

Spalding smiled at Frankie as he ushered his wife out of the dining room. He looked pleased with himself.

Frankie began to clear the table. With two martinis, nearly four glasses of wine, and now brandy, not to mention what she'd drunk earlier, Frankie doubted Mrs. Spalding would make it down to breakfast at seven.

She's a lush, Frankie thought, *worse than Momma ever was.* And the likelihood that only the undertaker would be there for breakfast made Frankie edgy.

Do Job, Get Food

Booze Town

Not Welcome

Streetcar

**Sleep in
Hay Loft**

Trucker

CHAPTER 6

Escape

"What?" Frankie mumbled sleepily. A breeze rattled the branches outside her open bedroom window. The smell of rain was in the air. She woke instantly and listened then sighed, realizing it was only the wind.

Why am I so jumpy? The door is locked. There isn't anything to be afraid of, is there? So Spalding was more friendly than she liked. *He can't get in, not with a chair under the door knob. Besides, he wouldn't do anything funny with his wife in the house, would he?*

Putting the thought out of her head, she peered at the luminous face of the alarm clock. *Four-thirty.* Could she go back to sleep? No. If she wanted to remain in Mrs. Spalding's employ, she had to figure out how to make bread—and before breakfast!

As she crawled out of bed, she heard a clap of thunder. *Boy, rain is all I need,* she thought. How could she get the clothes dry if it rained? She'd figure it out later.

Quickly, she slipped on her so-called uniform and glanced at herself in the mirror. Everything looked tidy except her hair. *Better get this out of the way,* she thought. She twisted her hair into a knot on top of her head and secured the curly red mass with bobby pins, something she'd seen her mother do before cleaning house. Except for her ratty tennies, she looked presentable and older than her thirteen years.

Determined to accomplish the impossible, she headed downstairs.

By the time the witching hour of seven rolled around, she'd botched and dumped one batch of bread dough and a second was rising. The table was set, coffee perking, crispy bacon in the oven. The pancake batter was ready for the griddle, and the orange juice was freshly squeezed.

Seven o'clock came and went. Frankie punched and kneaded the bread. By eight o'clock, it had risen and was in the oven. "Darn," she muttered, looking out the kitchen window. It had indeed begun to rain. "How am I going to dry the wash?" Sighing, she headed to the laundry room to find that Mrs. Spalding had one of those new-fangled washing machines and dryers she had seen in magazine ads. By nine o'clock, she had started a second load of washing and the first was in the dryer.

Surprisingly, the bread looked edible when she popped it out of the oven. It was after ten when she concluded the undertaker and his wife wouldn't be down for breakfast. Quickly she ate, cleaned the kitchen, and hurried down to the basement to finish the wash.

In the laundry room, she folded the second dryer load and started upstairs, arms laden with towels and bed linen. As she reached the top step, she heard Mrs. Spalding complaining loudly. She stopped to listen.

"Damn it, Charles!" Mrs. Spalding snapped, "I want a Bloody Mary. Where is that stupid girl?"

"Quiet, Helen." Spalding's voice was gentle and coaxing. "She might hear you. From the looks of things, she's done everything on your list. The bread smells delicious. I've got a feeling Frankie's going to be better than any of the girls you've ever had."

"I really don't give a damn, Charles. That's what she was hired for. All I want is a Bloody Mary and if I don't...."

Banging open the door, Frankie rushed into the kitchen, hoping they hadn't realized she'd been eavesdropping.

The woman scowled. "Damn it, girl, you can do the laundry later. I want a Bloody Mary, now!" She peered at Frankie's bundle. "And put the laundry away."

Frankie blinked, startled by the woman's outburst. As always, Mrs. Spalding was beautifully groomed, but Frankie could see that the woman was hung over, red-eyed, and ill-tempered—much like Abigale after a binge.

Spalding raised an eyebrow as though to warn Frankie to "take it easy".

Jeez, Frankie thought. She swallowed hard and willed herself to be polite. "Yes, ma'am. Which do you want me to do first?"

"Don't be impertinent!" The woman's eyes flashed angrily. To Spalding she said, "You really must do something about this girl. She's unacceptable."

Frankie gulped, her mouth dry as chalk. *Is she going to fire me?* she wondered.

"Now, now, Helen," Spalding said. "Everything's going to be fine." He gave Frankie a reassuring smile over the top of his wife's head. "I'll fix you a Bloody Mary, then we'll have lunch." More to himself than to them, he said, "Hmm...yes, lunch in Fargo." He pondered a moment, studying Frankie. His smile broadened—a shiver shot up Frankie's spine. "In fact, Helen, let's make a night of it. I'll call the Hamilton and reserve a suite."

Helen Spalding brightened at his suggestion, then frowned. "But what about business?"

"I'll have Albert handle things while we're gone."

"And what about her?" she said, flicking a red-enameled finger toward Frankie. "If she steals anything, I'll have her arrested."

Huh...? Frankie thought. She couldn't believe her ears. *Steal something? What a crazy idea.*

"Darling, you know that won't happen," Spalding said, his voice sweet as honey. "Frankie comes highly recommended and she's much too responsible to do anything foolish. She wants to pay off her debt. Don't you, Frankie?" Frankie nodded, wide-eyed. Spalding continued, smiling pleasantly at his wife. "We haven't been to the Hamilton in weeks, darling. While you're packing a bag, I'll get your drink." To Frankie he mouthed, "Don't worry," and led his wife out of the kitchen.

51

Frankie stared blankly after them. What a mess she'd gotten herself into. But like Spalding had said, she was responsible for her mother's marker. Now she felt more obligated than ever. She squared her shoulders, determined she'd work things out.

Through the afternoon and early evening Frankie worked, the large house an oppressive reminder of Mrs. Spalding's threat. The house was filled with antiques, paintings, silver, and other valuables, the likes of which Frankie had never seen. The size of the place would have made cleaning it a challenge even for a grown woman, let alone a girl her age.

Near exhaustion, she completed her chores, glad she didn't have to prepare dinner as well. From the freshly baked bread, she made peanut butter and jelly sandwiches. She cut up an apple, poured a glass of milk, and went up to her room.

All afternoon she'd worried about her predicament. She knew she should talk to Mrs. O'Reilly, but kept talking herself out of it, not wanting to worry the woman.

She changed into jeans and a blue-plaid flannel shirt and flopped on the bed. Between bites of sandwich and sips of milk, she reread her father's letters and studied the photos intently. They comforted her. The reminder that she had a family soothed the sting of Mrs. Spalding's nastiness. With a sigh, she began to put everything back into her mother's satchel.

"What's this?" she wondered aloud, seeing the corner of a piece of paper tucked inside the lining. It wasn't another letter, but a birth certificate. Hers. Frances Jane Ross, born March 11, 1940. Weight, 9 lbs. 10 oz.

"I was fat," Frankie murmured. She smiled and continued to read. Mother's name: Abigale Margaret Ross. Father: Frank Thomas Cooper.

Something isn't right. Momma's name wasn't Ross, it was Cooper. I'm Frankie Cooper, not....

She stared at the document. *That couldn't be.* As if zapped by an electric shock, she dropped the certificate.

The document explained her father's letters and why Abigale didn't go home. Frankie's parents hadn't been married. She was illegitimate.

"Oh Momma," she cried. "Why didn't you tell me? I'd have understood." At least, she thought she would have. Tears trickled down her face as she wept for the mother who'd protected her by taking her father's name, and for the man who'd wanted to marry Abigale and died before he could. After a while, Frankie cried herself to sleep.

Much later, something brushed her cheek. She pushed it away and rolled over, groping for the covers. A familiar smell registered through the fog of sleep. *Spalding's aftershave? Can't be. He's in Fargo with his wife.*

Instantly she woke, realizing she'd forgotten to brace her chair under the doorknob, and that he was in her room. *The man must be crazy!* With all her concentration, she willed herself not to scream, feigning sleep. Through slightly opened eyelashes, she saw Spalding lean over. From his expression, Frankie knew he intended to kiss her.

She flipped onto her back, lifted her knees, and kicked with all her strength, knocking Spalding off balance. She was off the bed and halfway out the window when he grabbed her leg and yanked her back into the room.

"Oh no, you don't," he said, smothering her face with wet kisses and pinning her to the bed. His breath smelled of alcohol.

"NO!" Frankie screamed as she struggled to get away.

An ugly laugh echoed through the room. "Now, now," he said, tugging at her pants. "Other girls like it." He laughed again as he fumbled with the button on her jeans. "Helen doesn't like you. Gonna fire you. So it's now or never."

Rage overrode Frankie's terror. *No one's gonna to do this to me! Ever!* When his lips came down on hers again, she bit. Her stomach turned at the taste of blood.

"Bitch!" He knocked her off the bed, his hands flying to his mouth. In that split second, she scrambled to her feet and dove out the window, grabbing at branches as she slid down the roof.

"I'll get you!" he yelled after her.

Just before she went off the edge, she snagged a branch and held on until it broke. She tumbled into some lilac bushes. Scraped and bruised, she untangled herself and ran, thankful she hadn't broken or sprained an ankle.

In the distance, she heard a train. *Gotta get to the hotel!* her mind screamed. *Mr. Helman will hide me until Mrs. O'Reilly gets there. She'll know what to do.*

Gasping for breath, she stumbled up the back stairs of the hotel. *How can I explain what happened? Mrs. O'Reilly would believe me, but around town, it would be my word against the undertaker. And who would believe a kid?*

Then there is Mrs. Spalding. What if something valuable disappears from the house? Another thought popped into Frankie's head. *What if Spalding stole his own watch and pinned the theft on Jeanie to get rid of her?*

Wrestling with these thoughts, she sucked in a breath of air and continued up the stairs. The hallway was dark when she opened the back door. *Why isn't the light on? It's always left on at night so the old codgers won't fall if they have to use the bathroom. Still, it shouldn't be hard to find Helman's room, even in the dark.* She slipped through the doorway. Her heart skipped a beat when she caught the familiar scent of aftershave. *Spalding! He must have guessed I would come to the hotel.*

55

As she spun around, he grabbed her shirt sleeve and it ripped as she bounded down the stairs.

"Told you I'd get you, and I will!" he snarled, his voice menacing.

You gotta hide, Frankie told herself. But, where could she go? There wasn't anywhere he couldn't follow. Then she heard two short blasts of a whistle. *The train! Can I catch it before it pulls out of town? I have to try or...* she chopped off the rest of the thought. She sprinted down the alley, running faster than she'd ever run before.

As she rounded the corner at the station, she tripped and fell. Up ahead, in the moonlit railyard, a steam engine was coupling onto a string of boxcars. Behind her, Spalding's pounding footsteps were closer—a lot closer. She stumbled to her feet and ran for all she was worth, determined Spalding wouldn't catch her.

Find an open boxcar, her mind screamed. Her lungs felt like they would burst as she ran alongside the cars slowly rattling and clanking out of the yard. She glanced back. Spalding was gaining.

Then she saw what she needed. Three cars ahead of her was an open door. If she could only reach it, she'd be safe! The train was beginning to pick up speed, but somehow she managed to sprint. She ran alongside the open door. How could she possibly get inside the car? It was chest high and, even if she could belly-flop onto the floor, she might slip out and....

Spalding was closer.

No! He can't win now, not now, not when I'm so close to escaping. She kept even with the open door. *How can I jump in? I can't. It's too high.*

Just when all seemed lost, a man leaned out of the doorway. Above the clatter of the wheels she heard him yell, "Run, kid, run!"

She willed one last, final surge of speed. A strong hand grabbed her outstretched arm and pulled her into the boxcar, dumping her in a heap on the floor.

Stay Out Physical Harm

Liar's Home

Angry Man's Home

Kind Man

Hit the Rail

CHAPTER 7

Riding the Rails

"Whaddya steal, kid?" the man shouted above the noisy freight. He herded her along the wooden wall toward the front of the boxcar. The car swayed as the freight picked up speed and clickety-clacked along the track, making it difficult to keep her balance.

"Nothing," Frankie snapped. She rubbed her bruised shoulder. How dare he manhandle her and accuse her of stealing anything. He was almost as bad as the Spaldings. She knew she should thank him for saving her, but right now she was mad enough to spit nails.

"Better sit down, kid," he said, pulling her to the floor beside him. Sooty grit and icy air whistled up through cracks in the floorboards. She trembled, both from the cold and shock, which reminded her that all she had in the world was what she wore.

Momma's bag! she cried silently. Her father's letters and photos were gone, gone forever. No matter how much she wanted to cry, though, she wouldn't, couldn't, not in front of this strange man.

"If you didn't steal anything," he said, "why was that guy tryin' to catch you?"

How could she explain? It was too embarrassing. When she didn't answer, he continued, "Good thing this is a milk run. Slow as molasses. Another couple of minutes and she'd've pulled away without you. Lucky you didn't try to jump. You'd've never made it."

58

Frankie shivered, not wanting to be reminded.

The man lit a cigarette. The flame flickered out before Frankie got a good look at him. He took a drag. His tone matter of fact, not condescending. Had she heard his voice before? *Nah, couldn't be.*

Leaning forward, she rested her chin on her knees as she collected her thoughts. "Why'd you wait so long, mister?"

"I was dozin'. Must be two o'clock, or thereabouts. Lucky I was here. Don't like guys trying to hurt kids, even if they stole something."

"But I didn't steal anything!" she yelled.

"Okay, okay." He chuckled. "I can hear." Abruptly his voice sobered. "That fella was mighty determined to keep you from leaving Devils Lake."

Didn't Frankie know it. Recalling Spalding's reprehensible behavior was more than she could handle. She burst into tears.

"Damn." The man swore softly under his breath. "You're a girl."

"Un-huh," she hiccuped, her teeth began to chatter. "When Momma died, I wanted her to have a proper burial. I didn't know Mr. Spalding liked young girls."

The tale of her mother's death leading up to her flight from Spalding spilled out between sobs. The hobo took off his jacket and put it around her, ignoring her protest. Finally her tears subsided. She wiped her face and runny nose on the back of her hand. She waited for a response. When none came, she asked, "Don't you believe me?"

He handed her his bandana and, in the hazy moonlight through the open car door, she saw him nod. "Yep. I 'magine you're not the first girl he's pursued. Seen his kind around before."

He paused for a moment. "Grown women's one thing, but young girls're something else!"

He pulled out a bag of tobacco and began to roll a cigarette. "Your mom would be proud of you, kid. Real proud. Getting away from that weasel took some doin'. Now, where ya headed?"

Panic raced through her. Where was she going? There was Mrs. O'Reilly, of course, but being in the same town with Spalding was unthinkable. Somehow, she had to let Mrs. O'Reilly know what happened.

Then she remembered her father's letters and the clipping about his death. There was only one place she wanted to go. Sucking in a deep breath, she spit it out.

"Washington."

The hobo chuckled. "Hope you mean the state of Washington, 'cause if it's D.C., you're headed in the wrong direction."

"Huh?"

"Washington, D.C.'s southeast of here. This train's headed due west into Montana, Idaho, and Washington State."

Still slightly confused, she nodded. "Yes, that's where I am going. Washington State. That's where my grandparents live."

"Where in Washington?"

"Uh, I don't know." She chewed the inside of her lip. She wished she had the funeral notice and Momma's satchel. *Think*, she told herself. "Hmm.... There was a photo of my mom and dad, and blossoms. Apple blossoms?" She scrunched up her face, concentrating. "It's a funny-sounding name. All I remember is 'basket'. Like a basket of...apples?" She shrugged. "Sorry, I don't remember."

"It's okay," the man said. "The key is 'basket' and orchards. Shouldn't be too hard to figure out." One by one, he ran through the names of towns in Washington's apple-growing regions, first the Yakima Valley then the Wenatchee Valley. But with each name, Frankie shook her head.

"Okay, let's try the Okanogan Valley. Bridgeport? Brewster? Pateros? Omak? Tonasket?"

"That's it!" Frankie squealed. "Tonasket! A tisket, a tasket, a green and yellow basket, Tonasket."

The hobo grinned. "Pretty good, kid. Should've thought of that one, myself." He nodded. "I've been through there. Nice little town, lots of orchards. Never worked there. Worked in Omak at Biles & Coleman. Pulled and stacked lumber. Nice people up and down the valley."

61

He lit another cigarette, leaned his head against the rough wood, and was silent for a while. As the freight rocked steadily along, whistle blaring mournfully whenever it approached a remote country road, Frankie wondered what he was thinking.

Outside the car, the night sky faded to pearl gray, tinged with pink. In the half-light of dawn, a bemused expression crossed the man's face as he cocked his head and peered at Frankie.

Frankie stared into his smiling eyes. *He was the hobo. The blue-eyed hobo.* How ironic. He'd saved her again. Maybe there was a reason he'd appeared out of nowhere. She didn't understand why, but for some reason she felt safe.

"Well, I'll be," he said. "If it ain't Red. Never thought I'd see you again, kid." He scratched the stubble on his chin. "We got a problem, though. A big problem."

Frankie stared at him blankly. "What?"

"You being a girl."

"What's wrong with being a girl?"

"Questions. Hardly ever see a girl on the rails. Not fifteen- or sixteen-year olds, anyway."

"I'm thirteen."

"Whoa! That's even worse. The bulls—the railroad detectives—will sure be curious why I'm travelin' with such a young girl."

He shook his head. "It won't look good. Even the yardmen'll figure you for a runaway. Might get arrested. Now, if you didn't have all that hair, I could probably pass you off as a nephew or something."

Cut my hair? Her hand flew up to her thick, red locks. *What a ridiculous idea. Then I'll look like a boy. But, that is the general idea, isn't it?* She drew in a breath. "Okay, we'll cut it."

The man chuckled then frowned. "Are you sure?"

"It'll grow out." She hurried on before she changed her mind.

"You got a knife, mister?" She paused. "I'm Frankie Cooper. Who are you?"

"Blackie."

"Blackie. Blackie what?" She waited for him to say more, holding out her hand for the knife.

He appraised her quizzically. "You sure you really want to do this? Hackin' it off is goin' to hurt like the devil."

"No, but what else can I do?"

Blackie nodded, pulling a pocket knife from his jeans. He studied her hair. "Hmm. Red. Dakota Red. From now on, you're Dakota Red. Like I said, I'm Blackie. Blackie's my handle."

Frankie wasn't sure what a handle was, but with a little prodding, she was sure he'd explain. "Blackie for your hair?" she asked, glancing at his thick, black hair.

63

He chuckled, as though pleased by her perceptiveness. "Probably, though ironically my name is Black. Clarence Black. First time out, I got pinned Minnesota Blackie, 'cause I'm originally from Minnesota."

He removed his hat and ran a large hand through his hair. "And, because of this. Hobos only use their handle. So call me Blackie. Okay? Good."

Flipping open the knife, he lightly scraped his thumb over the edge. "Careful. It's sharp," he said, handing it to Frankie.

While she chopped off clumps of hair, Blackie told her about the town where her grandparents lived. Oh, how she wanted to get there. It sounded nice. Really nice. Finally, she'd hacked away the last strands. She swallowed hard. "Would you...uh...could you..." Her eyes brimmed with tears.

"Could I what, Red?"

"Could you help me get home? Would you, uh, ple-e-ase?"

He frowned. "Wasn't planning on going through Washington. Take you as far as Havre. Then I'm swinging up through Canada to Alaska. I'm gonna hire on with a fishing boat and pile up some money."

Frankie squinted, trying to remember the school's atlas of the United States, Canada, and the Alaska Territory. After a moment, she drew an outline in the air of the coastline between Alaska and the State of

Washington. "Couldn't you get to Alaska from Tonasket?"

"Yeah. I s'pose you're going to Tonasket whether I go with you or not?" She nodded and he chuckled, which she figured he often did. "You're one determined kid, Red." For a long minute he studied Frankie's face, as though she were someone else. A sad expression flickered across his face, then disappeared. "Could put you on a bus, but there's no guarantee your grandparents still live in Tonasket. Then what? Better make sure you find 'em. That's what I'd want a 'bo to do if you were my daughter."

Frankie sighed, and for a fleeting moment wondered if he had a family. *If he does, they're lucky. He seems like a nice man.*

"Riding the rails is dangerous and against the law. The chances of you making it alone ain't good."

The tone of his voice changed. Frankie knew he was serious. Dead serious. "All I ask is that you follow instructions. Keep your voice low, so people will think you're a boy. If anyone wants to know anything, lie. You're headed for Seattle, you lived in...South Dakota. Ran away 'cause your stepdad beat ya. You and me are going to make money fishing in Alaska. Got that?"

Frankie nodded.

Tired, rubbing his eyes, Blackie said, "I'm gonna get some sleep. Once we hit Minot, we'll get some grub and warmer clothes and a bedroll for you. Then we'll head on to Havre and jungle up by the river."

"Jungle up? What's that?"

"Hobo jungle. Where 'bos camp out. Swap stories, share food, coffee, cigarettes, booze." Frankie grimaced. *Does he drink like Momma and the Spaldings? But then, if he does, there isn't anything I can do about it. I have to get to Tonasket.* So, she kept her mouth shut and catnapped. Blackie woke her as they pulled into Minot, North Dakota.

"Bull here's a sonofagun. Gotta get off before we pull into the yard. Otherwise, Warski will be all over us asking questions. I'll go first. I'll be runnin' when I hit the ground. If I trip, I'll roll away from the train. Before you jump, watch for sign posts along the tracks or anything you might slam into. Do what I do, and you'll be okay. Got it?"

Frankie nodded, and watched as Blackie tossed his bedroll out and slipped out the door on the run. She followed.

It wasn't as easy as it looked. Landing slightly off balance, she began to fall, but managed to pitch forward into an awkward ball and roll away from the tracks and the wheels of the train.

Swiftly, Blackie had her on her feet fast and through a hole in a wood fence lined with chest-high brambles. Gently he pushed her to the ground. "Stay here. Gotta get my bedroll. Don't worry, I'll be back."

From her position behind the bushes, Frankie could see a green pickup truck moving slowly along the track. The driver scanned each car as he drove by.

Is he the bull? she wondered.

To her right, she saw Blackie watching the truck. The driver stopped, got out, and walked along the string of boxcars. As he walked, he stooped and peered under each one. He was getting closer to the car they'd been in when two hobos dropped to the roadbed farther along the track. The man leaped into his truck and sped after them.

"That was Warski," Blackie said a few minutes later, his bedroll draped over one shoulder. "He's a tough so 'n' so. Always on the watch for 'bos coming in. Doesn't care if you're leaving, though. Hope those guys got away. Otherwise, they'll be sitt'n in jail till mornin'."

"Really?"

"Yep, then Warski'll put them on the next freight and tell 'em not to come back. C'mon, Red. I got enough money for breakfast and a hair cut."

Frankie peered at him, puzzled.

"Not for me, for you. Hope a barber can salvage what's left. Looks pretty bad."

Her eyes widened with alarm.

"Don't worry, Red," he chuckled, "it'll grow. First, something to eat. Then the rest will take care of itself."

He shrugged his bedroll higher and they pushed their way through the weeds, away from the yard fence and a large "NO TRESPASSING" sign.

CHAPTER 8

A Friend

Blackie led the way to a small cafe on a sidestreet near the railyard. Then, pleasantly stuffed with ham, eggs, hashbrowns, and biscuits, Frankie tagged along as Blackie headed toward a barbershop.

"Who the hell cut your hair, kid?" the barber grumbled when Frankie climbed into the chair.

The reflection in the mirror almost made her want to laugh. On one side was the gap-toothed, middle-aged barber eyeing the mess she'd made with Blackie's pocketknife, over the rims of thick-lensed glasses. On the other side, Blackie was trying to keep a straight face. In the middle was Frankie with her clumps of hair and a puffy eye turning purple. What hair remained looked like it had been hacked off to undo the mischief of several packs of bubble gum.

When Frankie didn't reply, the man shrugged. "Well, I'll do what I can. Can't guarantee nothin', except it'll be short. Real short."

"Ain't Red's fault," Blackie told the man. "He told me I'd had too much to drink! 'Fraid I made a real mess of it. Do what you can."

Frankie winced. *Why did he have to mention drinking?* Sometime she'd tell him how much she hated it.

68

The barber studied her reflection. "Not often I cut a pretty boy's head." He ran his fingers through the uneven tufts of red curls. "Better keep it short, or folks might think you're a girl."

Frankie gulped.

"Just joshin', kid." He raised his hands defensively. "Didn't mean no offense. 'Sides, girls don't sport black eyes. Hope you whupped 'im good."

When Frankie opened her mouth, she saw Blackie frown and motion downward with his hand as a reminder to speak low. She inhaled slowly and, in a tone she thought a boy would use, mumbled, "Bloodied his nose." Blackie grinned a "you-did-okay-kid" kind of grin.

While the barber trimmed and shaped Frankie's hair, Blackie inquired, "The baker still selling day-old bread?"

"Yep," the man replied. "Raised the price, though. Ten cents a loaf. Bailey's Grocery's got a bin of old vegetables they'll sell for near nothin'. Free to 'bos after they close. Keep an eye on the butcher, though. Schroder'll try to pass on more gristle and fat than meat. But it's fresh and cheap. Free soup bones if you're broke."

He turned his attention back to Frankie. "Ain't much more I can do, young fella," he said, shaking out the cloth from around her neck.

Frankie stared at her reflection. *Well, he said it would be short. Not quite a crewcut, but close.*

The barber faced Blackie, "That'll be four bits."

Blackie dropped two quarters into the man's hand and steered Frankie out of the shop. Standing in the doorway, the barber watched them cross the street. He tugged at his lower lip. After a bit, he shrugged and ambled back into his shop.

Blackie glanced back at the barber over his shoulder as they walked. "We gotta be careful, Red."

Frankie stared up at him indignantly. "He didn't know I was a girl. I sounded like boy, didn't I?"

Blackie chuckled, eyes twinkling. "I'm not yelling at you, Red. The black eye threw him off, but we really gotta be careful, 'cause it would be just our luck if Warski or some yardman stopped us. A hat would help. The reason it would, my feisty friend, is you're pretty. Damn pretty. That butch-cut won't fool Warski for one minute if he gets a straight-on look at you."

He perused her clothes. "Yep, a hat, another shirt, boots, wool socks, gloves, and a warm jacket." He shifted his bedroll as though it were a reminder. "And a bedroll."

In the basement of the Salvation Army, Blackie pulled a gray wool shirt out of a large barrel of free jumble. Other than frayed elbows, it was in pretty good shape. He held it up to her, gave a nod, set it aside, and continued rummaging.

By the way he picked through the clothes, Frankie again wondered if he had a family. Before she could ask, he headed toward the stairs with the shirt and an old black sweater tucked under his arm. Upstairs he rounded up everything except a pair of boots. Until they could find another mission, her tennis shoes would have to do.

With Frankie in tow, Blackie walked to the front of the store. He leaned on the counter and smiled at the clerk, an elderly woman with wispy, blue-white hair. The woman was dressed in tailored gray slacks, a white cotton blouse and an old black cardigan sweater. "Miss Frazier, I'm back. Could you fix this?" He shoved the gray shirt toward her. "In exchange, I'll chop some wood and do whatever else you need done."

The tiny, bespectacled woman returned his affectionate smile. "Clarence, where have you been? My goodness, it's been ages since you've been by."

She paused a moment and peered inquisitively at Frankie. *Clarence?* Frankie thought, returning the woman's quizzical look. Obviously, the woman knew Blackie on a first-name basis and was as fond of him as he seemed to be of her. "Who's your young friend, my dear?"

The instant Blackie answered, Frankie knew by the expression on the woman's face he'd said the wrong thing. "Uh...nephew," he said, his face flushing slightly. "Frank Jenkins. Frankie, this is Miss Frazier. We've been friends a long time."

The woman smiled, then frowned slightly as she looked from Blackie to the girl. "Uhmn," she murmured. "I didn't know you had a nephew, Clarence.

71

Weren't you...?" Before he could reply, she hurried on. "Oh, he must be one of your in-laws' youngsters."

Blackie flinched and the old woman seemed to realize her blunder. "Oh, Clarence, I'm sorry. I didn't mean to remind you of Sarah and the children." Tears came to her eyes and she clamped a thin, blue-veined hand over her mouth.

"It's okay, Miss Frasier," Blackie said quietly, handing her a handkerchief.

Sniffling and wiping her eyes and glasses, she looked up at Blackie. "But I thought Sarah's family wasn't...." She bit off the rest and shook her head. "Forgive me, Clarence. I know you don't like talking about it."

She sighed, and took another tack. "Why don't you and Frankie come by for dinner. Fried chicken, mashed potatoes, gravy. And, of course, apple pie."

Suddenly a wave of loneliness washed over Frankie, remembering the night her mother died. She'd been eating apple pie and studying in the hotel cafe. She shivered, pushing the memory out of her mind. The disquieting thought vanished when Blackie accepted the old woman's invitation.

"How could we refuse, Miss Frazier?" He grinned at Frankie. "Miss Frazier spoils me. Apple pie is my favorite."

"Mine, too," replied Frankie, nodding her head enthusiastically.

Miss Frazier smiled. "Good. I have about everything I need. Clarence, if you'd kill a pullet and clean it for me, I'd appreciate it. While you're at it, rustle up some apples from the cellar. Won't take any time at all to make a pie."

"May I help, ma'am?" Frankie asked.

Miss Frazier lifted an eyebrow and smiled. "Didn't know boys like to make pies." She pursed her lips and looked from Frankie to the hobo. "Don't know how you got hooked up with Clarence or why, but I have a feeling I'll find out tonight."

She smiled at Blackie. "Why don't you and Frankie stay the night. No need to camp down by the river. Just make yourself at home. The back door's open, and I'll be home around four. For lunch, there's meat loaf for sandwiches and cookies in the cookie jar."

"Thanks, Miss Frazier. Can't stay tonight, 'cause we're heading for Havre." Blackie smiled. "You sure you don't need anything from the store?" She shook her head. "Okay. C'mon, kid. I need some smokes."

On their way though town, Blackie said little and an awkward silence settled between them. To make conversation, Frankie talked about her mother and their many moves, but he didn't seem to hear, his mind was elsewhere. Finally Frankie shut up and just walked, wondering what had happened to his family.

Paying for a bag of Bull Durham at a general store, Blackie said to Frankie, "We'll catch out tonight. Stash is getting low. Know a rancher in Havre who'll hire us 'fore we head out."

Frankie didn't know what "catching out" or "stash" meant. Blackie smiled when she frowned. "Sorry, Red," he said, stuffing the bag of tobacco and cigarette papers into his shirt pocket. "We'll catch a freight out of town late tonight. I'm running low on money. Could use some of my savings, but I've got that pegged to buy another farm come fall. We'll work a week or so in Havre, then move on. That's what I've been doing since...."

As he stuffed his change in his pocket, he suddenly stopped. He took a deep breath, then let it out slowly.

"I know you're wondering about what Miss Frazier said. It's hard for me to talk about. In fact, Miss Frazier's the only person I've ever told."

He took another breath. "Maybe it's time I accept what happened and move on." Tears filmed his eyes. "Let's get outta here." He nudged her toward the door. "I'll explain when we get to Miss Frazier's She's got a little place outside of town."

Frankie followed him, feeling strangely sad.

Later, in Miss Frazier's sunny kitchen, Blackie made a pot of coffee. "Might as well sit outside till it perks. After coffee, we'll tend to the chicken and get the apples." Motioning Frankie out the back door, he sat on the porch step and rolled a cigarette. Frankie sat down beside him, watching him intently. He took a long drag from the cigarette.

"Ironic how I met Miss Frazier. Spring of '48, it was. Woke up at the Sally sicker'n a dog. I was burning up with fever. Ached all over. Miss Frazier got some 'bos to move me over here. Turns out I had the mumps. Never been so sick in my life. I was out of my head for a while and said some things I normally wouldn't have."

His face softened at the memory. "Betsy and Nathan. Betsy would be about your age now." He smiled at Frankie. "You remind me a lot of her. Feisty little imp. Nathan would be eleven." He rolled another cigarette and lit it, looking off into another place and time. In a halting voice, he continued.

"Early November I went into town to buy feed and groceries. The truck threw an axle outside of town and I had to wait overnight for a part to fix it." He took a drag of smoke. "I hadn't rigged the line from the house to the barn yet. Weather was still mild. The line's so people don't get lost in a bad storm, and can get to the barn and back safely. An early blizzard blew through."

His voice fell to a whisper, and Frankie strained to listen. "Storm finally blew out three days later." Taking another drag of smoke, Blackie stared off into space. Tears glistened his eyes. "Sarah must've taken the kids with her to feed the stock, and do the milking. Kids loved to play with the cats.

"When they left the barn, it was dark, probably snow so thick you couldn't see your own hand. And a fierce driving wind had come up. That's prob'ly what warned Sarah to leave the barn." Blackie sucked in a breath and let it out slowly. "So they did. And because the line wasn't up yet, Sarah got disoriented. The house was only 100 yards away, but they missed it." He paused and then choked out the rest. "I found 'em down by the creek."

Before she could stop herself, Frankie stammered, "F-f-frozen?"

He looked off across the yard, his face grim. "Yes, they...they froze to death."

She didn't know what to say. Finally she said what she felt was true. "But it wasn't your fault, Blackie. It was...circumstances. Like with Momma. Yeah, she was drunk. But if the railing hadn't broke, she wouldn't have fallen. How could anyone blame you?"

"But they did."

"Who did?"

"Sarah's family. The Jenkins. Her parents wanted to string me up. They'd never wanted us to get married to begin with, me being an orphan my aunt took in, and all.

After the funeral, I tried to drown my sorrow. Late planting my crops. Finally, I just let the bank take the farm and hopped a freight."

Before Frankie knew it, she blurted out, "Do you still drink?"

Blackie seemed to understand her concern. "Miss Frazier got me straightened out. Rarely take a drink anymore, and never, never on the road."

Frankie sighed, hoping so.

CHAPTER 9

A Meal

When Miss Frazier came home, she bustled around the kitchen fixing supper. Frankie pitched in, peeling potatoes, setting the table and helping make the apple pie. While they ate, Blackie filled the elderly woman in on Frankie's situation. Miss Frazier didn't say much, but Frankie could sense the woman's sympathy with her predicament.

After dessert and when the dishes were done they sat on the back porch, Frankie on the steps, the hobo and the old woman on a swing. Frankie smiled when she saw Miss Frazier pat Blackie's hand.

"I'll keep quiet about you-know-what," the old woman said to Frankie, with a laugh. "Your being a girl.

She turned her attention to the hobo. "And Clarence, it's time you settled down. With this summer's fishing money, and what you've banked, there should be enough to make a down payment on a small place somewhere."

Her smile softened. "And, Frankie, don't worry about your grandparents. They are going to enjoy you as much as I do. You're a joy to have around."

Frankie felt a lump in her throat. If the Coopers liked her as much as this woman did, she surely would be accepted. Wouldn't she?

77

"Now, it's time you two were off," Miss Frazier said, rising to her feet. "Drop me a line and let me know how you're getting on." She patted her apron pocket. "And I'll mail your card to Mrs. O'Reilly, Frankie. She pondered a moment. More to herself than the others, she said, "In fact I just may deliver it myself. I always wondered why Alice Atwood's granddaughter quit working for Helen Spalding. Probably for the same reason Frankie left."

Blackie studied the woman. "What're you up to, Martha?"

"Me?" Her tone was innocent, but the look on her face was quite determined.

"Yes, Martha, you." He grinned. "I've got a feeling you're gonna raise some hell."

Miss Frazier's voice became steely. "You bet I am. That man should be strung up and his carcass left for the vultures. Frankie was lucky. Mighty lucky! The next girl to work for the Spaldings may not be. That scoundrel has to be stopped!"

"Maybe Frankie and I should...."

"No," she said firmly. "With Alice's help, we'll tend to it. She's on the schoolboard. And we'll put a stop to Charles Spalding's shenanigans."

Confident, she nodded her head. "You must get on your way, Clarence, find Frankie's folks and then head north. Now, it's getting late. You better be off."

Flapping her apron, she shooed them down the back steps and blew them kisses. At the end of the driveway,

78

they turned for one final wave. "Love ya," Blackie called, as they turned toward town and the freight yard.

A warm feeling washed over Frankie when she heard the old woman's response, "Me too, son."

For several minutes, they walked in silence. Frankie turned up her collar against the chilly night air, thankful Blackie had found the wool jacket for her. At least a size too big, the jacket didn't look like much, but with the gray shirt Miss Frazier had mended and the sweater, it was warm.

"You love Miss Frazier a lot, don't you?" Frankie said.

"Yeah." Blackie's voice was soft. "She's the only real family I ever had. Mom died when I was born. Don't know who my father was. Aunt took me in. Uncle didn't want me 'cause they already had nine kids to feed. In '37, I hit the road. Worked on farms, orchards, for the railroad, sawmills, in the woods—anything for a few bucks. Miss Frazier's more like a mom than my aunt ever was."

He rolled a cigarette and lit the wooden match with a thumbnail. "And she's notorious for setting things to rights. When she gets through with Spalding, he'll be history. You can bet on that."

"But what if no one believes her?" Frankie asked. "It may take some doing, but if anyone can convince them, it's Miss Frazier. Everyone respects her. See, she used to be the grade school principal in Devils Lake and they know what she stands for. Spalding's done in that town."

He rambled on. "It's too bad she chose to be a spinster, 'cause she would've made a wonderful mom. After she retired, she moved here to take care of her mother. Miss Frazier took up volunteering at the Sally and has befriended more 'bos than I can count."

"What happened to her mother?"

"Died a few years back."

Blackie fell silent as they approached the railyard. A gust of wind pelted them with damp soot from an engine that chugged a short distance to the east. They skirted the dimly-lit depot and slipped through a hole in the fence.

"Keep an eye out for a switchman," Blackie said. "He can tell us where the train for Havre's being made up."

On the far side of the yard, Frankie heard a locomotive shunting cars. The hobo headed up the track in the direction of the sound, and she hurried after him.

As they drew closer, Frankie saw a shadowy outline. She squinted, trying to figure out whether it was a man or a sign. She tugged at Blackie's sleeve and pointed across the tracks. "I think there's a guy over there."

"Where?" he asked, peering into the darkness.

"There." Pointing, she stepped over the rail onto the track. In that split second, she knew she'd made a mistake. A phantom-like mass bore down on her and she froze. Before she could scream, Blackie had grabbed her arm and flung her off the tracks. A single car ghosted past, silent and dark as the night.

Spitting out soot and dirt, Frankie scrambled to her feet. Shaking uncontrollably, she began to cry.

"It's okay, kid," Blackie said softly. He leaned over as though to hug her, seemed to have second thoughts, and handed her his bandana instead. Frankie would have liked the hug, but knew he hesitated because of what had happened with Spalding. She sniffed, and wiped her eyes.

"I've had a couple close calls myself," he said. "When they're switching cars to make up a string, one of the cars they've cut loose can drift hundreds of yards." He jammed his hands into his pockets. "Wasn't your fault. I should've told you the rules of the road."

He covered the essentials and finished with, "Like I said, riding the rails is dangerous. Always, always, stop. Look. And listen. When you're not sure, do what I do. If we run into anybody, let me do the talking. Oh, and if we ever get separated, I'll look for you in the next town we're headed for. Okay?" Frankie nodded. Blackie swore under his breath, as a long freight rattled past, blocking their way.

Frankie could still hear cars being switched from one track to another. "How're we going to get over there?" She pointed to the other side of the freight, now rumbling to a stop.

"Walk around. But if the string's too long, we'll find a flatcar and cross over. C'mon."

After they'd walked past twenty or more cars, Blackie elected to cross over. Spying a flatcar, he walked to mid-span and swung up onto its floor. He clambered to his feet and crouched down to help Frankie aboard. Frankie grabbed his hand and he lifted her topside. Quickly, they crossed its open flat surface and dropped to the roadbed on the opposite side.

As Frankie started after Blackie, she felt a large hand clamp down on her shoulder. "Where you fellas headed?" a gravelly voice asked.

"Havre," Blackie shouted over the din of a passing yard-engine.

In the shadowy light of the moon, Frankie could see the man holding her wasn't dressed like a railroad bull. He wore coveralls. *A switchman?* His fingers bit painfully into her shoulder.

The man shined his lantern in her face. "Take off your hat, kid," he ordered.

Frankie's insides quivered. She pulled off her hat, keeping her face as blank as possible.

"Curly red hair," the man said to no one in particular. "Green eyes. Tall. Skinny. Pretty like a girl. 'Cept for the short hair and black eye, you fit the description."

"Whaddya mean, description?" Blackie demanded from behind the man's shoulder.

"Runaway. Some girl, working for the undertaker over in Devils Lake, stole his wife's diamond earrings." He waved a flyer. "This bulletin says she hopped a freight last night. Undertaker almost caught her, 'cept some 'bo helped her get away. Maybe the girl was you, eh kid?"

Frankie's stomach lurched. She glanced at Blackie. How was he going to talk them out of this?

"Ah, c'mon," Blackie said. "Does Red look like a girl? He's good-looking, but hell, he ain't that good looking."

The man flicked the beam of the lantern across Frankie's face again. "Yeah, he could be a girl. Damn right he could be." He laughed, a nasty, rasping sound, and the hairs on the back of Frankie's neck prickled.

"And I know how we can find out," the man said with a guffaw. "Drop your drawers, kid."

Free Food

Nice Lady

Hot Yard

Beware Police

CHAPTER 10

The Test

Drop my drawers? Pull my pants down? She couldn't believe what she was hearing! Did he think she was crazy? The idea was too absurd even to consider.

Blackie chuckled, adding to the affront. "Red's got nothing to hide, have ya kid? Do what the man says." Frankie felt his eyes boring into her, willing her to obey.

How could Blackie expect this of me! But, I'd promised I'd do what he said. "Sure," she muttered through clenched teeth. Her face burned, and it took all her willpower to undo the metal button of her jeans. Feeling beads of sweat on her lip, she tugged at the zipper.

The man laughed. "Forget it, kid. I believe you." He laughed again. "No girl'd drop her drawers. No way."

"Where's the Havre freight being made up?" Blackie shouted as Frankie sighed with relief.

The yardman pointed behind her, toward the train which was still shunting cars. "The Havre run's being made up on track five, but you got a wait. Won't be pulling out for another hour or so."

As the man walked away, he laughed again. "Sorry about the mix-up kid. Guess it was the hundred-dollar reward that got me hoping you was that girl."

"What?" Frankie gasped.

The man stopped, turned, and walked back toward them. "Whaddya say?" he yelled.

Frankie shook her head, glad the clanking of the freight had masked her voice.

"I said, a hundred bucks is a lot of money," Blackie called.

The man stopped in front of Blackie, tapping the lantern against his leg. "Yeah, that undertaker's wife must want the girl real bad. Wouldn't want to be in her shoes. With that bulletin out on her, bulls'll be looking for her from here to Seattle."

"Mmm," Blackie muttered. "Red and I could use a hundred bucks. We'll keep our eyes peeled."

The man laughed. "Do you no good if I see her first." He walked off, whistling.

After the man disappeared up the tracks into the dark, Frankie stared at the hobo. "It's a lie," she yelped. "I didn't steal anything."

"I know, kid, I know. You told me. It's probably a smoke screen Spalding uses. Miss Frazier said her friend's granddaughter left for some unknown reason. Wouldn't be surprised if every time a girl leaves, something turns up missing."

"Yeah," Frankie said. "Mrs. Spalding said she'd have me arrested if anything disappeared. So it's probably happened before."

"Not surprised," he said. "Well, there's nothing we can do about that now. We'll wait and see what Miss Frazier finds out. Let's find an empty and stay outta sight."

As they walked the line of cars, Blackie said, "I never ride with anyone I don't know. If someone crowds in on us, we'll find another car. Safer that way."

He stopped and looked at her. "And till we get this straightened out, try not to talk, okay? Pretend you're hoarse."

Frankie nodded. That wouldn't be hard. With all the shouting she'd done on the train, her voice did feel hoarse.

They stopped at a car that appeared empty, but in the front end, two cigarettes glowed. Down the line, they found another that looked unoccupied. Blackie was in and out of the car in seconds.

"Fool," Blackie muttered, and moved on.

Frankie hurried to catch up. "Who is?"

"Guy in that last car." Blackie glanced back at it over his shoulder. "Drunk as a skunk. Won't be long till he meets his Maker."

"His Maker?" Frankie asked. "You mean, dies?"

"Yep. Stupid to drink and ride the rails. You saw yourself tonight how risky riding is. If you're drinking, the odds go up twenty-fold."

After a few more cars, they found an empty and climbed in. Blackie pinned the door open with a railroad spike.

"Why'd you do that?" Frankie asked.

"So the door won't slam shut on us. Knew a couple of 'bos in Wyoming who forgot to pin the door. Train slowed sudden for some reason, and the door slammed shut on them."

He shook his head in caution. "You can't open the door from the inside. Car they were in got switched off to a siding along the way. Took three days before they cut through the wood floor with their pocketknives. Ran out of water and near died of thirst."

Riding the rails was becoming more complicated by the minute. What other horrors awaited them? Goosebumps galloped up her spine.

"Now, you wait here while I find some cardboard," the hobo said. He moved to the far end of the car, where he tossed his bedroll. "We'll keep you hidden till we get outta here. Just because we fooled that switchman doesn't mean we can push our luck."

"Okay," Frankie said. But she wasn't crazy about the idea of being left alone. "But, why do we need cardboard?"

"It cushions the ride and it's cleaner. I won't be long." He was gone before she could ask what she should do if anyone tried to commandeer their car. She hunkered down in a corner. For several minutes she fretted about what she should do if someone tried to take their boxcar. *Stop it,* she told herself. *Blackie will be back any minute and he won't let anything happen.* Feeling more secure she dozed briefly, to be startled awake by the sound of two angry men's voices approaching the car.

"Damnit, Muskrat," one said, "did you have to lose the whole roll?"

"I-I-I...could...couldn't...help it, Preacher," the other stuttered. An explosion of foul language followed. The voices grew louder and stopped in front of the open boxcar door.

Frankie studied the men in the moonlight. They were in their late twenties and as opposite as night and day. The tramp that stuttered was hulking with as much dark, curly hair on his face as he had on his head. A filthy red and white bandana was knotted around his head. He had to be the one called Muskrat. Both wore clothes much like those Frankie had seen in the Sally's jumble bin. Muskrat's companion was short and wiry. A battered brown hat covered dirty blonde hair and a pockmarked face. He chewed on the stub of a cigar. An ugly red scar sliced through a mustache into a stubbled chin. Frankie shivered. She was sure Blackie wouldn't ride with him or Muskrat. *Time to bail out!* Heart pounding in her throat, she picked up both bedrolls and crept to the door on the opposite side of the car. There was just enough room to squeeze through. As she pushed the pack out, something thumped on the floorboards. Glancing back, she saw the hairy man climb into the car.

Her nose wrinkled with disgust. She'd smelled offensive body odors before, but Muskrat was the rankest. Preacher swung up into the car, too. He didn't smell much better. He peered at her in a way that was unsettling.

"Well now," Preacher said, moving toward her, the cigar moving from one side of his mouth to the other. Springing out of the car, she dropped to the ground.

"Hey," he called after her, "if ya got a bottle, you can ride with us."

Like heck, she thought. Snatching up the bedrolls, she headed down the tracks. *Now what?* She stopped for a second to get her bearings. She had to find Blackie, but he was on the other side of the freight, which meant she'd have to walk around the end of the train. Or cross over a flatcar, which she didn't want to do. Calculating she had about a half hour before the freight pulled out, she set off again at a labored trot.

As she approached the caboose, she saw a brakeman climb aboard. A second man started back along the track, checking each car with a lantern. She could smell smoke in the air, and the rumble of steam engines farther down the track. The freight would be pulling out soon. *Where is Blackie?* She looked around but couldn't see him. Time was getting short. If she wanted to find him, she'd better move faster.

She hurried up to the caboose. "Hey, mister, have you seen my partner?"

The brakeman, leaning from the platform, shrugged. "Seen five, six guys tonight. What's he look like?"

"Tall. Black hair. Old, gray hat."

"Which means like 'most every 'bo hereabouts," the man said with a laugh.

He was right. In the dark, Blackie wouldn't look much different than the other hobos she'd seen around the Sally in Devils Lake. A thought popped into her head.

"Cardboard. He was looking for cardboard."

"Oh, that guy. Yeah, I saw him. You must be the kid he was looking for. Told us if he couldn't find you, he'd be in that gondola."

He pointed toward what looked like a boxcar cut in half. "Better climb on, kid. Steam's up, and once Delbert finishes checkin' the rest of the string, we're highballin'."

"Thanks, mister."

Frankie hurried for the gondola, struggled up the ladder, and dropped the bedrolls over the wall. Two sharp blasts pierced the night, and she dropped over the side just as the car jerked forward, pitching her across the car and into a corner. Dazed, Frankie rubbed her scraped elbows and knees. She looked around.

Where is Blackie?

Beat It

Don't Enter

CHAPTER 11

A Job

Frankie struggled to her feet. The car swayed and finally smoothed out as the train picked up speed, and she clung to the gondola's sill to maintain her balance. The hobo had to be in the car somewhere.

"Blackie," she called, "where a-a-are you?" The words disappeared under the clickety-clack of the wheels. The moon cast shadows inside the open space.

"Blackie?" she called again, thinking she saw him in a far corner of the car. Slowly she edged forward along the sill.

"Where are you?" she wailed, when the shadow proved to be just that, a shadow. She bit her lip to keep from crying, but tears came anyway. What was she going to do? Blackie wouldn't leave without her, would he?

The freight was bound for Havre, Montana, and if Blackie wasn't somewhere on it, she was on her own. Without his help, finding her grandparents, or avoiding getting caught, would be next to impossible.

Sniffing, she made her way back to the bedrolls, stuffed them in a corner and sat down to mull over her plight. A glimmer of moonlight filtered through the thin clouds. "Well, at least it isn't raining," she mused. "And there's no way I could get locked in."

Pangs of fear and loneliness crept over her as she unrolled her bedroll and crawled in. Each jolt of the train accentuated her worry of ever rejoining Blackie. Rocked and jostled by the swaying car, she fell into a sleep frequently disturbed by the cry of the steam engine's whistle as the freight approached each crossing.

The whistle's wail woke her before dawn. Stiff and sore, she climbed to her feet as the train rumbled on. The rush of air was chilly. The night was fading to pearly gray, tinged with pink. In the half-light of dawn she looked out over a sea of rolling fields. A quarter mile ahead of her, two steam engines strained under their load. Black smoke rose in billowing wispy plumes across the fading moon.

The train slowed to a stop on a siding in Glasco, Montana. Frankie leaned over the sill of the car, hoping to see Blackie standing in one of the other gondolas or walking down the tracks looking for her. For over two hours she watched, ducking down whenever a yardman appeared.

Not until the train was again underway and nearing Havre, did Frankie accept that Blackie and she had indeed been split up. Until he caught up with her—and she prayed he would—she had to get off the freight in one piece without being stopped by a bull.

But how? The gondola had no doorway for her to jump from. She'd have to be really careful climbing down the ladder, and then be ready to drop off and run for it if a bull spotted her.

Then there was the problem of the bedrolls. She'd have to pitch them out before the train hit the yard, then walk back and get them. If she could find them.

The freight began to slow down. The engineer was leaning on the whistle and ringing a bell to announce their arrival. When they reached the outskirts of town, she flung the bedrolls out and watched them roll down an embankment into tall weeds. As the train rumbled toward the yard, she counted telephone poles from the spot where they'd landed.

Frightened, Frankie straddled the sill. The train passed a grove of cottonwood trees and she caught glimpses of a river. The sight of the track rolling below made her dizzy. She closed her eyes and swallowed. *Maybe I should just stay in the car until it comes to a full stop,* she thought.

Can't, she told herself. *Bulls will be looking for me.* She inhaled deeply and forced herself to grab the ladder. Her hand slipped. "Damn!" She swore under her breath, wiping her sweaty hands on her jeans. Heart pounding wildly, she grabbed the ladder again, swung over and edged downward. *You can do it,* she told herself, clinging to a step as the freight slowed to a fast walking speed.

Up the track, a man was walking in her direction, peering into every empty boxcar. He hadn't spotted her yet. She had to get out fast.

Gingerly, she turned to face the trees. Holding her breath, she leaped outward. Somehow landing on her feet, she dashed into the cottonwoods and brush surrounding the freight yard. As she rolled under a bush, she saw the bull motion the tramp called Muskrat and his partner out of the car they'd commandeered.

She flopped down on her stomach in the weeds to watch. She saw the man hand Muskrat a sheet of paper. *Cripes,* she mused. *Is that a reward poster? Another bull? Probably.* His attire was like the bull in Minot. She watched as Muskrat shrugged and passed the flyer to Preacher. He also shrugged, looked at it and started to hand it back, then looked at it again. The bull nodded. Apparently, Preacher asked to keep it, for he stuffed it in a pocket of his torn denim jacket.

"Jeez!" she muttered. "Now they'll be looking for me, too." She watched the tramps move off toward the river, each carrying a gunny sack. The bull walked toward the caboose and climbed aboard. A few minutes later the brakeman came out on the platform and pointed toward the gondola she'd just vacated. The bull nodded, and checked the car. Shivers ran up Frankie's spine. *Boy, that was close.*

Her stomach grumbled loudly. *What am I going to do for food?* Going into town was out of the question. She didn't have any money and, besides, the bull might see her. *Maybe there is something in Blackie's bedroll.*

Frankie stayed hidden while cars were switched to other tracks and new cars were added to the freight she'd been on. For more than an hour she watched the bull patrol the yard. Finally the freight pulled out westbound. The man watched it leave, then crossed the tracks and entered the depot.

Frankie crept farther away from the yard and, under cover of the trees and brush, worked her way back to the bedrolls.

She looked around. Where could she go? She was covered with soot and grime, and wanted desperately to wash. *Go down to the river,* she told herself. She had to stay away from the jungle, or she'd run into Muskrat and his friend.

Shouldering both bedrolls, she cut toward the river, on the watch for a place to lay up. Upstream, smoke spiraled through the trees. *That must be the jungle,* she thought. She turned and walked in the opposite direction. When she figured she was nearly a mile from the hobo camp, she washed up, then settled under a fir tree with boughs that nearly touched the ground.

Rifling through Blackie's pack wasn't something she wanted to do, but she needed food. Inside his bedroll she found a change of clothes, his shaving kit, a small skillet, tin plate and cup, a can opener and spoon. She remembered his pocketknife she'd used to hack off her hair. Her eyes misted. *Where are you, Blackie?*

Alongside a can of pork and beans, several slices of stale bread, and a Hershey bar, she found a photo album. She opened the cover.

"Oh," she murmured, peering at photos of a pretty blonde woman. When she flipped to the next page, there was the woman with Blackie. *This must be Sarah,* Frankie thought.

She leafed through the pages filled with photos of Blackie and Sarah and their two children. Nathan had his mother's curly, blonde hair, but Betsy's had been dark, like Blackie's.

The pictures showed a happy family, like the images she imagined when she let her longings surface. Her eyes stung. *Why'd they have to die? It was unfair. So, so unfair.* She brushed at her tears and went through the album again, realizing there were no photos before or after Sarah—as though Blackie hadn't existed before his family or after. An empty feeling ran through her as she thought ahead. *Will I ever find my grandparents? And if I do, will they accept me, an illegitimate grandchild? Or just tell me to "move on," like the bulls did with hobos?*

It was too depressing to think about. Somehow, by the time she got to Tonasket, she had to come up with a plan to convince her grandparents they'd want her. But, if Blackie didn't show up, it probably wouldn't matter anyway. She'd get caught, arrested, and….

The rest vanished when she heard the wail of a locomotive in the distance. Quickly, she opened the can of beans and ate half, saving the rest for later.

Eyes peeled for the bull, Frankie crept back to the freight yard. She watched from behind some brambles as a westbound passenger train pulled in and departed. There was no sign of Blackie.

All that day and into the next evening, with every westbound train, Frankie repeated the pattern, to no avail. The last of the food was gone, and her stomach complained. *What can I do?* She supposed she could go to the Salvation Army dining hall. The Sally always fed down-and-outers. *No, I might run into Muskrat and his crony there,* she reasoned.

She'd seen derelicts scavenge food out of trash cans in the alley behind the Zigfelt Hotel, but she wouldn't stoop to that. She could always wash dishes in exchange for a meal, but where? Some little, out-of-the-way cafe where nobody would be looking for her would be best. *I'd better clean up so I'll be presentable.*

After taking a bar of soap from Blackie's shaving kit, she found a spot along the river, secluded and overgrown with reeds. Checking to make sure no one was around, she bathed and washed her hair. The short, bristly hair on her fingertips felt as though she were scrubbing a stranger's head. After dressing, she set out for town. As she skirted the yard, she kept watch for anyone who might take an interest in her, but no one seemed to pay any attention to her.

The manager of the first cafe Frankie tried for a job didn't need a dishwasher. The next two eateries suggested she try the mission. On a sidestreet, she hesitated outside the Sun Woon Chinese Restaurant. The door stood open to the sidewalk, and an appealing, exotic mixture of smells wafted out.

Mouth watering, Frankie peeked in. An Oriental woman, dressed in dark baggy slacks and a jacket, served the tables, all occupied. Three young Oriental children studied and played quietly in a corner booth. Beyond a partly curtained doorway to the kitchen, she saw a short, middle-aged man preparing food quickly while dishing up several plates at the same time. She was amazed at how swift and efficient he was. Taking a deep breath, Frankie went inside, determined not to be turned down again. She walked straight through the cafe and into the kitchen.

The Chinese man looked up from his work, blinked, and barked in broken English, "What you want?"

"A job," Frankie said, inspecting the kitchen. Apart from the cook, there was only a frail, old woman washing dishes. Frankie plunged ahead in the sing-song voice of the man. "I help mother wash pots and pans. Do dishes. Chop vegetables. Scrub floor. Empty trash."

The cook stared at her, and Frankie held her breath. Finally, he grinned. "Okay. All you want eat and four-bits."

He said something to the old woman that Frankie didn't understand. The woman smiled, nodded, dried her hands, and shuffled into the dining area. Frankie went to work.

She'd never worked so furiously in her life. By the time the dinner rush ended, Frankie was ravenous and was mopping her sweaty brow with a dish towel.

"You do good," the man said. "Now we eat."

"We?" she asked, surprised she'd be included. She'd expected to have to eat in the kitchen, alone, as she had done at the Spaldings.

He nodded. "Yes. You, me, wifey, mother and children. You like what I fix. Fried rice."

Frankie didn't know what fried rice was, but anything would be welcomed. Her stomach grumbled loudly.

He nodded. "You hungry. I fix special chicken. Very good. You like. You watch."

For the next few minutes, Frankie watched him assemble a fragrant, piping-hot meal. Her stomach grumbled louder. She wished he'd hurry up. She was starved.

"How you get black eye?" he asked, tossing vegetables into a wok.

"My stepfather hit me," Frankie lied.

"You run away?"

Frankie nodded.

Sun Woon continued asking questions, most of which Frankie dodged.

Later, in the dining room, after Frankie had finished her dinner, she licked her lips and sighed.

"You like?" the man asked.

"Oh yes! It was wonderful."

"You eat Chinese before?"

She shook her head no.

"Tomorrow I teach use chopsticks." He cocked his head, looking at her thoughtfully. "You be careful, missy. Riding rails very not safe. You make dead fast."

Frankie gulped, "How did you know?" Abruptly, she shut up. On the sidewalk outside the window, arguing loudly about whether to buy a bottle of wine or chow mein, stood Muskrat and his cohort.

Cheap Labor

Protected House

Beware Two Dogs

Barking Dog

CHAPTER 12

Ellie Mae

Frankie gulped, scrunching down in the booth. A quizzical look crossed Sun Woon's face. His mother said something Frankie didn't understand and he looked above her into the long, rectangular mirror directly over her head. From his expression, she knew he could see the reflection of the two tramps arguing outside the cafe window.

"I take care problem," Sun Woon said. He barked instructions to his mother, wife and children. In unison they stood, the children retreating into the kitchen and the women chattering and clearing the table while the man watched the mirror.

"Under table, missy. I close restaurant."

Frankie slid to the floor, peering around the end of the booth and the woman's baggy pants, holding her breath. *Don't come in,* she pleaded silently. *Go away.*

Suddenly, she felt clammy. *Did Preacher get a good look at me when they commandeered my boxcar? Probably. There'd been enough light in the yard. Will he figure out I am the girl the bull was looking for, even with my short hair? Probably.*

She shuddered. *A hundred dollar reward is something the tramps won't pass up.*

All of a sudden, Muskrat moved toward the restaurant door to look inside. "Preach...er, I'm hungry!" he complained loudly.

An explosion of profanity echoed into the cafe when his companion grabbed Muskrat's ratty collar and pulled him down the street.

Even before Sun Woon could close the door, Frankie bolted into the kitchen and out the back door. She wanted to thank the man, but couldn't chance the tramps returning. For a hundred dollars, they might do anything.

As she raced down the alley toward the freight yard, she heard the bang and clatter of cars being shunted. She circled the yard, cautiously crossed the tracks and returned to her hiding place to resume her vigil for Blackie.

As she watched, her panic subsided and exhaustion washed over her. *Jeez,* she thought, struggling to stay awake. *I better not fall asleep.* She leaned against the trunk of a cottonwood tree and closed her eyes.

Several minutes later, the sound of cars slamming into one another woke her. Yawning, she peered through the weeds and saw two hobos drop out of a boxcar. Then another jumped from a car farther down the line. All three headed in the direction of the jungle.

The lone hobo walked slightly bowlegged, like Blackie. Was it him? "Bla..." she started to call. She managed to chop off the rest. She had to be cautious. She couldn't get caught. Slowly she crept forward for a better look. The glow from the yard lights showed a tall, dark-haired, muscular man wearing a hat and wearing the same kind of jacket Blackie wore.

How could she be sure? The 'bo was too far away for her to see his face. He was carrying something. A bed roll? She had Blackie's bedroll, so maybe this wasn't him. But, if it was, she had to make sure. The only way she could find out would be to follow the man.

Do I dare risk it? Goosebumps prickled her scalp as she remembered Muskrat and Preacher. She couldn't have slept long. They must still be in town. If she was careful, really careful, nobody would see her. Finding Blackie was worth any risk.

"It's going to be okay," she whispered, trying to reassure herself. Quickly she got to her feet. She skirted the yard, watchful, and followed the men to the camp by the river. She felt like a mouse circling a trap as she crept near the perimeter of the hobo jungle.

Five ramshackle huts of cardboard and tarpaper over castoff wood skirted a dying campfire. With sagging roofs and leaning walls, they looked as flimsy as houses of playing cards .

A toothless, disheveled old man with a scraggly beard sat on an upturned, five-gallon lard can. Light reflected off the man's wire-rimmed glasses. A mangy old sheepdog slept at his feet. Around the fire, several other cans were used as furniture along with a sofa oozing stuffing. Its broken back was propped against a tree trunk lined with pots and pans and other cooking utensils.

The man tossed sticks of wood on the fire, and sparks flared up past two large coffee cans on an old refrigerator grill over the flames. The man seemed to recognize two of the three hobos she'd seen get off the train. He raised an arm and waved them toward the fire.

A heavyset barefoot woman emerged from one of the shacks, and lumbered off toward the river. Frankie shivered. *Are these shacks homes for the man and woman? Are there more people in the others?*

Suddenly, Frankie realized the lone hobo wasn't there. *Where did he go?* She crept closer.

The two men exchanged greetings with the old man, who dished watery stew from one of the coffee cans into tin cups and handed them to the newcomers. *Where is the other hobo?* Frustrated, she inched closer for a better look.

"Whaddya think you're doin'?" a voice rasped. A vise-like hand clamped onto Frankie's forearm. She stifled a yelp.

She couldn't tell if the Southern-sounding voice was male or female, but she knew it wasn't Muskrat or Preacher. One sniff confirmed that.

She forced herself to turn and look. Relief washed over her when she realized it was the woman she'd seen come out of the shack. But she cringed when she saw the woman's face. It had been badly burned. Ugly scars ran down the right side of her face and neck, disappearing under a dingy long-sleeved man's work shirt, draped over dark baggy pants. Long strands of brown hair partially hid a sightless eye and some of the scars.

"Sorry, ma'am," she gulped, trying to keep the horror out of her voice. "Looking for my partner. We got split up."

"Where?" the woman demanded, eyeing Frankie suspiciously. She ignored Frankie's reaction to her face, as though it were a daily occurrence.

"Uh..." Frankie stammered, her mind racing in search of an answer. With all that had happened, mentioning Devils Lake and Minot were out. "Caught out in Milwaukee. Blackie and I repaired rails in Fargo," she improvised.

"Minnesota Blackie?" The woman scowled, the expression making her face even more grotesque. Frankie's trembling worsened.

"Yes, ma'am. At least, I think so. But it might not be the same man."

"What's he look like?" The woman's grip on Frankie's arm tightened as if she harbored some pent-up anger.

Frankie flinched. *What'd Blackie do?* she wondered. Had he caused the woman's horrible burns?

"Didn't you hear me, kid?" the woman snarled, her fingers biting deeper into Frankie's arm.

Frankie was tempted to kick her and try to get away, but sensed that the woman could break her arm with a single twist. Through gritted teeth she said, "He's tall, black hair...blue eyes. Blue like the sky."

"Around thirty-two, thirty-three?"

Frankie thought for a moment. "Yes, ma'am." She was about to add, *about how old my dad would be if he hadn't died,* when the woman let go of her arm.

"Never knowed Blackie to travel with anybody," the woman said. She studied Frankie closely. "Don't mean he mightn't, mind you."

A smile flickered across her face as though at a pleasant memory. The smile was transforming and, for a moment, Frankie forgot how hideously disfigured the woman was. *This woman had once been pretty, perhaps even beautiful. What had happened to her?*

"Ain't seen Blackie in quite a spell," the woman said. "There's another train in a couple, three hours. Next one comes near daybreak. You're welcome to set a piece while you wait."

Frankie was in a quandary. *What if one of these hobos has heard about me? Or worse, what if Muskrat and Preacher come back to jungle up and see me? It's too risky.*

"Thanks, ma'am," she said, "but I'll wait over by the yard."

The woman ignored what Frankie said. "My name's Ellie Mae." She snorted. "Behind my back, some call me Scarface. They think I don't know, but I do. What's yours?"

Things were getting complicated. Next thing Frankie would know, she'd be telling her how she got burned.

"What's your name, kid?" Ellie Mae repeated.

Frankie gulped. "Red, ma'am. Dakota Red."

"Figures, with your hair. You a runaway?"

Goosebumps leaped up Frankie's arms. "Uh…" she stammered.

"Know how it is," the woman said matter-of-factly. "Ran away myself a few times. Stepma used to whup me good. Used pa's belt. Wouldn't've been so bad if'n it were only the belt, but the buckle hurt."

"What…" Frankie stammered. "Why'd she do that?"

"'Fore the fire, I were right pretty," Ellie Mae said, staring off toward the campfire as if looking into another time. She patted her ample bosom and chuckled. "But once I got these, all hell broke loose. Pa ran moonshine. Ma, she ran off more boys that I could count. I got reg'lar beatin's, 'cause I liked kissin' and stuff. Lived in the Great Smokies, we did."

She laughed. "Girl there ain't worth her salt if'n she ain't married by fourteen. I weren't much more'n thirteen, but I had my eye on Clabe Henry. Things were goin' good, till Pa started makin' eyes at me hisself.

Then my stepma beat the livin' daylights outta me and Pa both. Busted Pa's nose."

Frankie stared at the woman, trying to comprehend what she was being told. Before she thought, she blurted, "Did your stepmother cause..." Involuntarily, she touched her own face.

"Nah, weren't like that a'tall. If'n I hadn't fought back, none of it would've happened. Five little 'uns was all a-screamin' and Pa was tryin' to git the belt away from Ma. She popped 'im a good one. Buckle sliced clean to his cheekbone. Bellowed like a bull, he did, and sent Ma flyin' ass-over-teakettle into the table. Kerosene lamp exploded when it hit the floor, flames went ever' which way. Never thought a place could burn so fast."

She sighed. "I got the young 'uns out, though. Started back inside for Ma and Pa. They was still fightin' when a beam come down on me. Don't remember after that. They say my stepbrother drug me clear of our shack. Pa and Ma never made it."

Frankie grimaced, feeling sick to her stomach. "I'm sorry, ma'am." The tale was so bizarre it had to be true. The woman's scarred face was proof.

As they walked into camp and neared the fire, Ellie Mae asked, "Anyone seen Minnesota Blackie?" She flopped down on the mangled sofa. A bottle of cheap wine was being passed around. The dog raised a graying eyebrow briefly, then went back to sleep.

"Nope," one of the 'bos said. He wiped his mouth across his tattered sleeve and handed the bottle to Ellie Mae. She took a swig and passed it to Frankie.

Frankie didn't know what to do. No way was she going to drink any of the foul-smelling stuff. She took the bottle and passed it on.

"You too uppity to drink my booze?" the old, toothless hobo demanded, struggling to his feet.

"Steamer Jack, you ol' fool, leave the kid alone," Ellie Mae barked.

The hobo grumbled and shuffled toward Frankie anyway.

"You heard the lady," a quiet male voice said. "If the kid doesn't wanna drink, it's his business."

Flooded with relief at hearing his voice, Frankie sighed, "Blackie!"

Nice Lady, Sad Story

Beware of Cowards

}

Someone Home

CHAPTER 13

Partners Reunited

As Blackie circled the fire, Frankie started to jump up, wanting to throw her arms around him. The hobo shook his head, and motioned her to sit down. For a moment she had forgotten she was suposed to be a boy. A boy wouldn't do such a silly thing. Unhappily she sat down again, commanding herself to keep quiet. *Where had Blackie been?* she wondered.

He had a small flour sack slung over his shoulder and was carrying a string bag of oranges. Dropping the sack by the sofa, he handed the oranges to Ellie Mae. "Thought you might like these."

"You never forget, do ya?" she said, her face flushed with pleasure. As she reached to take the bag, it slipped from her grasp.

"Sorry," Blackie said, catching it and setting it on her lap. In the darkness, Frankie hadn't noticed the woman's left hand before. Now she saw that it was a web of scar tissue, and missing two fingers.

Frankie's eyes shifted from the woman's hand to her face and then down to her bare feet. Three toes on Ellie Mae's right foot were fused together too. Frankie grimaced, wondering what other scars lay under the long-sleeved shirt and baggy pants. If Blackie noticed how awful she looked, he didn't let on.

"Want one?" Blackie asked Ellie Mae quietly, sitting down beside her. She nodded and beamed like a child waiting for Santa. He pulled out his pocketknife and cut a hole in the bag. As he peeled an orange for her, Ellie Mae handed oranges to the others around the fire. The citrus aroma from the fruit was mouthwatering.

Frankie held hers for a moment, watching the motley group. *They're kind of like a family,* she mused. Not really a family, but she could see that the hobos shared whatever they had, be it coffee, stew, cigarettes, or booze. Or a bag of oranges. She thought it was like any other family. There were some people you liked and some you didn't.

The group around the fire grew quiet as they peeled the fruit, tossing the peelings into the coals and eating the oranges section by juicy section. Steamer Jack gummed his orange with great fervor. Ellie Mae smacked her lips, licking them and her mangled fingers as juice ran down her chin.

"Thanks, Blackie," she said softly.

"My pleasure, Ellie Mae." He got to his feet, motioning to Frankie. "Red and I've got a long day coming up, so we'll be turning in."

"Where you headed?" she asked.

"Going out to Pete Alexander's place at first light. Thanks for looking after Red. We'll see you next week before we catch out." As he turned to leave, the woman caught his sleeve, pulled him close, and whispered something in his ear. Then she patted his cheek and said, "Thanks again, Blackie."

Moonlight shimmered on the river as they ambled along, the flour sack over Blackie's shoulder. He stopped to roll a cigarette, smiling at Frankie's upturned questioning face. "I know kid. You're busting to find out what happened. And I'm proud of you for keeping quiet back at the jungle, 'cause one of the others would have guessed what Ellie knew right off, that you're a girl. That's what she whispered to me. She'd never give us away, but she doesn't think you can pull it off for long."

Frankie rolled her green eyes. "I've been careful." She switched subjects, anxious to find out what had happened. "Okay, what happened? Where've you been?"

"In jail."

"What!"

His match flared and she looked close to see if he were joking. He wasn't. Blackie nodded. "Yep. Warski arrested me just as the freight was pulling out. Spent the night in jail. He'd asked some locals about us. The barber pegged me for the 'bo helping you get out of Devils Lake. Said he'd wondered all along if you were a girl. When he saw your picture, removed some hair, and added the black eye, he was sure."

He took a drag of smoke and sat down on a log. Frankie could hear the murmur of the river, and far off, a coyote howl.

She felt sad. He'd helped her and look where it got him—in jail. "What did you do?" she asked.

"The only thing I could do. I called Miss Frazier to bail me out. She called the Devils Lake sheriff and after he checked it out, I got released. Seems after he talked with Mrs. Spalding, she found the earrings you supposedly stole, in Spalding's office."

"I knew it!" Frankie squealed. "I just knew it."

"Miss Frazier had him pegged right. For some reason the sheriff in Devils Lake wanted me to identify Spalding as the guy who tried to pull you off the freight. Seems there was another complaint. But by the time Miss Frazier and I got there, Spalding had taken off."

"You went back?" Frankie gasped. Tears of gratitude welled up and she giggled with relief.

"Yep," he said. "And Miss Frazier talked Mrs. Spalding into writing off your mother's burial and gravestone."

"Really? I don't owe anything to the funeral home?"

"Not a cent. And Mrs. Spalding won't be needing this." He handed her the flour sack.

She looked inside. Amid some clothing and shaving gear was her mother's satchel. She drew it out and hugged it to her chest. "Thanks," she whispered. "Now I have proof."

"Proof? Proof of what?"

"Of...of...." *Blackie would understand. But, maybe not? If he knew I was illegitimate it might change things.* She knew the thought was stupid but after all that had happened she was afraid to take the chance.

She had to get home. She smiled half-heartedly. "It's just that without Dad's stuff, the pictures and papers and things, the Coopers might not really believe I'm their granddaughter. Know what I mean?"

Blackie frowned. "Can't imagine why they wouldn't." He chuckled. "Stop worrying. They'll believe you."

He took a final drag of his cigarette and looked around. "By the way, where're our bedrolls?"

"That way." She pointed down the river toward a grove of fir trees.

"Well, I don't know about you," he said, "but I could use some sleep. We'll hitchhike out to Alexander's place first thing in the morning. He'll put us to work." As they maneuvered through the underbrush to Frankie's hiding place, he told her they would be mucking out barns, branding calves, repairing fences and other ranch chores.

"Good spot," Blackie said when they arrived at her hidden campsite. He untied his bedroll and spread it out under the tree. "See you found the beans and stuff." He frowned, then looked up at her.

"For crying out loud, you must be starved if that's all you ate."

Frankie smiled smugly, and he cocked his head.

"All right, 'fess up. What'd you do for eats?"

"Washed dishes and ate fried rice."

He pondered a moment. "Only fried rice is at the Sun Woon Restaurant," Blackie said. "Sun's makes great chow."

"Yeah! And he even said he'd teach me how to use chopsticks," she said. "Miss Frazier's chicken was good, but Sun Woon's was even better."

"Yeah," Blackie chuckled. "We'll swing by and see them before we catch out. Now get some sleep, kid."

Blackie crawled into his bedroll fully clothed. Frankie followed suit, using her jacket as a pillow. It seemed as if she'd just closed her eyes when Blackie gently shook her shoulder. "What time is it?" she mumbled sleepily.

"Five o'clock. I'd let you sleep, but life on a ranch starts early. You wash up and whatever else while I take care of the bedrolls. Here. You might need this." He handed her a roll of toilet paper. He didn't seem to notice her blush. "There's a cafe near the yard where we can get breakfast. Shake a leg, kid."

Frankie nodded sleepily, rubbed her eyes and headed for the river shrouded in the pre-morning light.

O   O   O

For the next week they mended fences, strung barbed wire, mucked out barns, and fed cattle. Late Saturday afternoon the rancher dropped them off at the railroad station. "Wish I could talk you and your nephew into staying, Blackie," he said "You're one of the best hands I've ever had. And it isn't often I get a boy who works as hard as this kid."

If you only knew, Frankie thought.

"Yeah," Blackie agreed. "Thanks anyway, Pete. If we couldn't make more fishing, we might." He gave Frankie an approving glance.

The rancher's pickup rattled into gear. "Hope things work out for you up north," he called. "If not, come on back and I'll put you both to work. See ya." He waved and drove off.

Frankie watched him drive away. "Then we'd have to tell him I'm a girl."

"Yep," Blackie chuckled. "For awhile there I wasn't sure we'd pull it off...you being a boy, I mean. But we did."

Blackie clapped her on the shoulder. "C'mon, kid. We need supplies for the road. Food, tobacco, another water canteen. Then some of Sun Woon's chicken and fried rice." They completed their errands and slipped through the back door into the fragrant smells of the Chinese restaurant.

"Missy!" Sun Wood exclaimed. "When you run off, we worry. Not know what happen." He looked from the girl to Blackie, grinned, then rattled off something to his mother, who stood at the sink cleaning vegetables.

"Blackie your friend?" he asked Frankie, bobbing his head with approval. Sun Woon's elderly mother patted Blackie's arm and said something to him. Sun Woon beamed as he translated. "Mother say she glad girl have you friend. She worry girl okay. Trains not safe."

Sun Woon's grin broadened. "But now missy safe. We celebrate. Catch fish morning. Fix good. Teach chopsticks."

A happy feeling swept through Frankie as they ate dinner. She missed her mother, but Blackie's friends had treated her as she imagined and hoped her grandparents would someday. Miss Frazier. Pitiful but gentle Ellie Mae. Sun Woon's family. No matter where Blackie went, he seemed to have "family" who cared about him, and he them. *Someday,* she thought. *Someday.*

"That was mighty good, Sun Woon," Blackie said later, sliding his chair away from a table crowded with dishes still heaped with food. "Would it be too much trouble to package what's left for a friend over at the jungle?"

"Not trouble," Sun Woon said. From the kitchen he brought several containers which he filled.

"For Ellie Mae?" Frankie asked, after they'd bid the family good-bye. The night was chilly as they started across the tracks back to the hobo camp.

Blackie nodded. "I've tried to get her to come into town with me but she refuses. I suppose it's understandable. Been taking her Sun Woon's chow now and again going on five years."

"Why doesn't she live with her family?" Frankie asked, lengthening her stride to keep up with Blackie's slightly bowed long legs.

He shrugged. "Probably the same reason I hit the road. After her father and stepmother died, she was blamed for the fire." He paused, his expression thoughtful. "Folks shunned her, and to add salt to her wounds, the boy she was crazy about couldn't stand the sight of her."

He sighed. "Her grandmother took Ellie Mae and her brothers and sisters in, but once Ellie's burns healed, her grandmother told her to git. She drifted around begging, riding the rails. Ended up here."

Ellie Mae's grandmother wouldn't let her stay? Frankie thought, panicking. *Will my grandparents tell me to "git," too? No, I'll just have to convince them not to.*

Another question struck her. "How does Ellie Mae live? I mean, she doesn't work, does she?"

"Nope. Steamer Jack and other 'bos give her most of the food she needs. As for the rest, there's the Sally, and.... Well, let's just say she gets by."

Frankie frowned. That wasn't much of an answer, but she'd learned hobos were close-mouthed about one another. One of the rules of their world. She put Ellie Mae out of her mind.

As they approached the campfire Frankie saw the silhouette of a hobo sitting on one of the large cans, playing a harmonica. The tune was sad, yet oddly soothing.

In the flickering light Steamer Jack and three other scruffy men played penny-ante poker at a makeshift table of lard cans topped with a plank of wood. Ellie Mae was nowhere to be seen.

"Ellie around?" Blackie asked. He paused in the shadows outside the campfire. "Got something for her."

"That you, Blackie?" the woman called, pushing past a blanket which served as a door to her shack. The ragged edge of the blanket caught on a protruding nail, enabling Frankie to see inside.

On a broken-backed chair sat a kerosene lamp, its light revealing a thin mattress and rumpled covers. The bed sat on cinder blocks and planks above a hard-packed, dirt floor. The bottom of an apple box, topped with cardboard served as a table, its surface littered with sardine cans overflowing with cigarette butts. A small caboose coal stove stood in a back corner to heat the shanty in winter. A clothesline hung across the room, the frayed towels draped over it partially concealed a man's back.

The man sat on the edge of the bed, pulling on his boots. Frankie flinched when he turned toward the door.

It was Muskrat.

Jail

Sleep In Barn

Mean Dog

CHAPTER 14

Trouble

Muskrat! If he's here, so's Preacher. Where? Frankie glanced around, her heart thumping like a frightened rabbit. *Why am I afraid? I'm not a wanted person anymore. But Preacher wouldn't know that.*

As she turned toward the fire, the harmonica player swiveled toward them. It was Preacher. He studied Frankie, his bushy mustache worming over the harmonica slowly. Now the tune he played was haunting and eerie. Shivers spiraled up Frankie's spine, whether from the sound of the harmonica or from the man's cold, snake-like eyes, she wasn't sure.

Why hadn't they left? Did they lay over to work? Somehow she couldn't imagine either of the tramps working anywhere. They seemed more likely to panhandle than work. Or had they waited around, hoping to catch her? Even though her imagination was working triple time, she felt the sooner she and Blackie got out of there, the better. She tugged on the hobo's sleeve.

"Blackie?" she whispered.

"Yeah, Red?" He glanced down at her.

"Let's get outta here." Her eyes darted from Preacher to the shack. "They're the two guys the bull talked to."

"Hmm," he murmured. "Seen 'em a time or two. And you're right, they're trouble. Especially that so-called Preacher fella. He ain't anymore a preacher than I'm Santa Claus."

He swore softly under his breath. "This might get hairy. Stick close, okay?"

Frankie nodded. She could feel sweat popping out on her upper lip.

"Catchin' out tonight?" Ellie Mae asked. She walked up to Blackie, eyeing the bag. "That for me?" She reached out to take it.

"Yep," Blackie replied, carefully placing the sack in the woman's outstretched, scarred hands. "Red and I thought some Chinese would hit the spot."

"Wh...What you got?" Muskrat asked, stepping out of the shack, frayed shirt tails flapping. His T-shirt looked almost as dirty as the ground he walked on. Taking the last swig of wine from a bottle, he flipped it into the weeds behind the shack.

Before the woman could reply, Muskrat reached over her shoulder and took the sack. Ellie Mae's eyes widened. She looked like a little girl who'd lost her favorite doll and, for a moment Frankie wondered whether the woman was going to cry or lose her temper.

But Ellie Mae had her own way of handling the problem. She swung around to face the tramp. The old sheepdog rose, growling. Steamer Jack spoke to it and the dog sank to the ground again. Blackie started to say something. She cut him off. Swearing, Ellie

Mae advanced on Muskrat. "Who the hell do you think you are, you no-good pile of horse manure!" she yelled, snatching the bag out of Muskrat's hands.

Frankie felt a giggle coming on, but it vanished as quickly as it had come when the tramp grabbed for the bag. Ellie Mae sidestepped, heading toward the fire.

"Gim...gimme that!" A jumble of stuttered profanity spewed out of the man's mouth.

Steamer Jack and his cronies seemed to know trouble when they saw it. They quickly pocketed their coins and faded into the shadows to watch. The dog followed. The night was suddenly quiet except for the frogs, crickets, and the crackling of the fire.

Muskrat and Ellie Mae circled one another like wary animals. In the flickering firelight, Muskrat's crooked teeth and eyes glittered. Determined to keep her prize, Ellie May clutched the sack to her vast bosom and began to back away.

Muskrat lunged for the bag, snagging it with one hand. As the bag tore, the cartons of food fell to the ground. Ellie Mae and Muskrat pushed and shoved like two small kids fighting over the last piece of chocolate cake. Frankie might have thought it funny if it hadn't been so frightening.

"Leave the damn woman alone!" Preacher snarled.

"Huh?" Muskrat muttered, stopping abruptly. A befuddled expression crossed his dark hairy face. He shook his head as though he hadn't heard correctly and continued advancing toward Ellie Mae.

"I said, leave her alone," Preacher repeated. This time his voice was ice-cold and adamant.

Muskrat sniffed the air like a hungry dog. "Ah, c'mon, Preacher, I'm starved."

"We'll get something later," Preacher said.

"But we ain't got no money."

Blackie put his hand on Frankie's shoulder. "Follow me if anything happens," he said quietly. Frankie nodded.

Preacher stood, pulled a partially-smoked cigar from his jacket pocket and then dropped the harmonica into it. He clamped the cigar to the side of his mouth and gave his partner a disarming smile. "Got enough for Chinese, since you're wanting Chinese," Preacher offered.

Muskrat brightened at the suggestion, then frowned. "Where...where'd you get the money. I thought...."

"Playin' cards, stupid."

"I...I ain't stupid," Muskrat growled, clenching hairy fists. He lumbered toward Preacher, scowling. He looked like an ill-tempered ape, and a hundred pounds heavier than his cohort. "Don't ca...call me that. I ain't dumb."

"Okay, okay," Preacher said, laughing and backing away. His eyes shifted from Blackie to Frankie and then to Ellie Mae. The cigar moved as his eyes shifted from one person to the next. "Sorry, ma'am," he said. "Muskrat didn't mean no harm."

"Then get the jackass outta here!" the woman snarled.

"Yes, ma'am." Preacher's eye moved from the woman back to Blackie and then settled on Frankie. He gave her a slow, crooked smile. "Like I said, Muskrat meant no offense."

Frankie's skin prickled under his watchful eye. She didn't like the way he looked at her. *Has he figured out who I am? Nah,* she concluded when his eye shifted to his partner. "C'mon," he said to Muskrat. "Let's get some chow mein." He gave Frankie another crooked smile and added, "God keep you out of harm's way." Muskrat licked his lips, and they headed toward town.

"That wasn't so bad," Frankie said, watching them disappear into the dark.

"Hmm," Blackie murmured, following her gaze. His face was thoughtful. Frankie could almost hear the hobo's mind whirring in thought.

"What's the matter?" she asked. "He didn't figure out who I am. Even if he did, I'm not wanted anymore. 'Sides, he wished us no harm."

"Maybe so," he said, still looking off in the direction they had gone. "I may be wrong, but I got a hunch Preacher's up to something."

While they were talking, Ellie Mae, Steamer Jack and the others joined them.

"That there Preacher ain't won nothin' from us," Steamer Jack said. "Lost a couple bucks, in fact. Think he's near broke. Better be watchin' out for him. Roll you, like as not."

Ellie Mae nodded. "Muskrat's kinda slow. But he weren't too bad till he hooked up with that Preacher feller. Sometimes, like tonight, Preacher's nice as can be. Then he'll turn meaner'n a rattlesnake. Better you git on down the line 'fore they come back."

"Yeah," Blackie agreed, "I think you're right, Ellie Mae. Red and I are out on the next freight. From the sound of things, it's bein' made up now."

Frankie heard the distant rumble of an engine and the cars being shunted in the yard. The sounds beckoned her and all she wanted was for them to be on the freight, safe and rolling west, away from the tramps and headed toward home.

Blackie patted the woman's shoulder. "And don't you worry none. Red and I'll be careful."

"Make sure them two don't waylay you in some boxcar," Steamer Jack said.

Frankie shuddered. The comforting thoughts of "home" evaporated.

Safe Camp

Catch Out Here

CHAPTER 15

Sharing

"What if they follow us?" Frankie hurried after Blackie through the dark cottonwoods, her eyes darting from shadow to shadow between the trees. *Are the tramps lying in wait?* she wondered.

"Like I told Ellie Mae," Blackie replied as they reached the perimeter of the yard, "we'll be careful."

In the light of a half-moon, Blackie peered at an engine idling across the yard. "Looks like diesel engines will be hauling us over the Divide tonight. Won't be long till steam engines are a thing of the past.

"Now let's find an empty. Don't worry about those tramps, kid. If worse comes to worst, we'll bail out. Fair enough?"

"Yeah." Frankie gave the woods another searching glance, and followed Blackie along the line of cars. They found an empty mid-span and climbed in.

While Frankie dropped their packs in the front end, Blackie pegged the door open. In a pile of cardboard trash he found a piece of two-by-four and laid it next to the wall, across from the door. "Now," he said, placing cardboard beside it, "if those two do show up, we've got something to fend 'em off with." He rolled and lit a cigarette, and for the next two hours they waited, backs against the side wall, tense and watchful.

A 'bo poked his head through the open door, and Frankie started. "Hello, there. Seen the coals of yer smoke. Mind if I ride with you?"

"Yes," was all Blackie said, and the man moved on up the line.

A few minutes later a brakeman stuck his head inside. "Remember, no fires. We're outta here in five minutes."

"Fires?" Frankie asked after he'd gone and they'd moved to the front end of the car.

"Gets cold riding over the Continental Divide. That's why I got the wool shirt and sweater at the Sally. With them and your jacket, you should be warm enough."

A rush of excitement washed over Frankie. *I'm getting closer,* she thought. *I'm gonna make it home.*

Blackie took a final drag from his cigarette. "Sometimes 'bos start fires in buckets to keep warm." He snorted. "Occasionally, it's on the floorboards of the car. Hoggers and brakies keep an eye out for hotboxes, too."

"What are hoggers and brakies?"

"Hoggers are the engineers. Brakies—brakemen. Hotboxes happen when the grease rags—they're in the journal boxes that lubricate the axle bearings—get overheated. That can cause a fire, even derailment."

After crushing out his cigarette, he pushed the butt through a crack in the wood floor. "Last year a couple 'bos had a fire get away from 'em. By the time the railies—the crew—got it under control, they'd lost three cars, two of 'em filled with wheat."

"What happened to the 'bos?" Frankie asked.

Blackie shrugged. "Imagine they headed for the river till the railies put the fire out and cleaned up the mess. Probably caught out on the same train, or maybe hoofed it to the next siding to catch another freight."

He stretched out his legs and crossed his ankles. "The Great Northern don't hassle 'bos much. 'Cept when they do something stupid, like setting a fire. Or breaking into a car and stealing stuff. Or maybe jumping from car to car."

He leaned back, locking his hands behind his head. "Now other roads'll throw you in jail just for trespassing. But James Hill, who built the Great Northern, had a vision for this country. He figured trains were the backbone of the nation. He also figured that they could provide jobs and move everything from lettuce to steel, from one place to another. Moving men to work those jobs, too."

He yawned. "Nowadays, migrant workers who don't have money to pay for a ride still catch out so they can go where the work is, from the lettuce fields in California to the apple orchards in Washington. When the railroads were being built, the Indians thought the engine was an iron horse and the tracks an iron road." He smiled at her. "Guess you could say we're taking the Iron Road Home."

Frankie smiled, warmed by the thought. *Home. I'm going home.*

Blackie dug around in his jacket pocket for paper and tobacco, and rolled another smoke. "But I'm afraid the hobo is a dying breed."

"Why's that?"

"Cars, mostly. Since the war, more people can afford them. It's easier for folks to move from place to place, so they don't need trains to get around. And 'bos, who ride the rails and work for food and necessities— well, we're being replaced by tramps, bums and winos. Men who travel but won't work, even if somebody offers 'em a job. Like Muskrat and Preacher."

Why wouldn't somebody want to work if they were offered an honest job? It seemed strange to Frankie. No matter how bad things had been, Abigale had always worked. First it was as a housekeeper for a rancher in eastern Washington, later at the hospital in Devils Lake. Even Frankie, young as she was, had worked helping clean up around the hotel, and in the hotel's restaurant in exchange for her dinner. "Where are you going to buy a farm?" Frankie asked, changing subjects.

Blackie struck a wooden match on the seam of his Levis and lit his cigarette. The match flared briefly, illuminating his faint smile. "Hmm," he murmured. Frankie felt rather than saw him gazing at her. "Hadn't much thought about it till you came along."

"Why's that?" she asked.

"Figured I'd decide when I got enough money saved. As it happens, I really liked the Okanogan Valley—where you're headed. I was there several years ago."

"Oh?" She liked the sound of that. For several moments she waited. When he didn't say anything, she prodded, "Well?"

"Worked at a sawmill in Omak one spring through the apple harvest. Beautiful orchards, lots of space. Nice people."

"Did you ever go back?"

"Nope. Just kept moving on. Wasn't comfortable being very long or very often in one spot back then."

"Would you feel comfortable in one place now?"

Again she felt him gazing at her. Finally he said, "Don't know, kid. But the right place, yeah—maybe so."

The engine gave two short whistles and the train jerked forward. They were on their way. Frankie exhaled deeply, confident they'd seen the last of Muskrat and Preacher. She leaned back against the wall and closed her eyes. She wondered where Blackie would find a place. *Tonasket maybe?* She would like that a lot.

During the next several hours Frankie slept, lulled by the clickety-clack of the car over the rails. Sometime during the night, Blackie settled her into her bedroll. Once, when the freight pulled onto a siding to let another train pass, she woke. Looking up, she saw him leaning against the doorjamb smoking a cigarette, as though standing guard. She went back to sleep, feeling safe.

The next time she woke, Blackie was snoring softly, propped in a corner of the car. Quietly she got to her feet and moved to the open door. As the train rumbled along, she noticed her breath made fleeting puffs in the frosty air. She shivered, glad she had the extra clothes Blackie had bought. She pulled her collar up over her ears. She peered out as the freight rumbled past jagged, snowy peaks that loomed above wooded hillsides so steep they seemed to tumble onto the track. She had no idea where they were in the Rockies, but the scene from the doorway was breathtaking.

"Better sit down, or hold onto the doorjamb," Blackie said, yawning deeply. "If we stop sudden, you could get pitched out."

Frankie dropped to the floor. "Thanks," she said.

He smiled. "You're welcome. By the way, another rule of the road is to stay out of the doorway when passing through towns. Kids sometimes throw rocks."

Then he rose and stretched, moving along the wall to sit beside her. He began rolling a cigarette. "I love this part of the country. Clean water, fresh air. Great fishing and hunting. If I didn't like orchards, I'd settle here."

Orchards! He likes orchards. Frankie thought. *Maybe, just maybe....*

A faint smile touched his lips as he lit the cigarette. "The thing I like about your grandparents' neck of the woods is the apple trees. It's beautiful this time of year. The valley'll be in full bloom." He paused. "Sarah and I had three apple trees."

"You did?" Frankie said.

He turned toward her. "Yep. In fact, the apple trees were Sarah's idea. We planted the first one to celebrate swinging the deal for our farm. The other two were to celebrate Betsy's and Nathan's births." Sadness clouded his eyes.

Before Frankie could stop herself, she blurted, "I've got a photo of Mom and Dad in an orchard." She wasn't sure why she was telling him, but she thought he'd be interested.

"Mind showing me?"

"Un-uh." She went to the flour sack, got the satchel, and settled down beside him again. Proudly, she handed him the photographs. He studied the pictures closely before setting them aside and picking up the book.

Darn, she thought. *What if he finds my birth certificate?* It was tucked in the back of the book. *Maybe he wouldn't notice it. But if he did, would it matter?*

"Kipling is a favorite of mine, too," he said, browsing through the book. "Hmm." The document slipped out and before Frankie could stop him, he unfolded it and began to read.

After a moment he chuckled. "You had fat little feet, like Betsy's." He pointed to the bottom of the certificate where her baby footprint had been recorded.

She smiled. "Now they're long and skinny." She peered at her sneakers, grimy and full of holes. "I wish the Sally'd had some boots that fit me."

"Darn it!" Blackie slapped his knee. "Knew I forgot something. I planned to buy you a pair before we left Havre. If we have to walk any distance, we got problems." He studied her big toe protruding from her left shoe. "Guess we'll have to call these your Sunday shoes—all holey." He winked and she laughed, her concern about her birth certificate forgotten.

He gazed out the doorway. "Hope we pull off pretty soon. I could use a stretch. Until we can get you a pair of boots, I better wrap some tape around your shoes. While we're at it, line both of them with the money Pete gave you. I've got my money in mine."

"Why?" It seemed like a peculiar place to carry money.

"Like Steamer Jack said, it's easy to get rolled."

"Rolled?"

"Robbed. Men like Muskrat and Preacher live by preying on unwary 'bos."

Frankie frowned. She'd forgotten about the tramps. "Is that why you stayed awake last night?"

"Partly. The sooner I get you home to your grandparents, the better."

He picked up the satchel and headed for the bedrolls. "C'mon," he said, sitting down. "Let's fix those shoes." As Frankie pulled off her shoes, Blackie got a small

133

roll of electrician's tape from his shaving kit. "Are you afraid your grandparents won't accept you because your parents weren't married?"

She felt the blood drain from her face. She hoped he hadn't noticed. *Jeez,* she thought. She didn't know what to say, so she said nothing.

"There's nothing to be ashamed of, kid," he said gently. "There were lots of people during the war who wanted to get married, but couldn't because of circumstances."

"Like my Dad not being able to get home before his ship sailed? I found a letter saying he couldn't."

Blackie nodded. "When I got shipped out, there were several guys like your dad. Some of them made it back, others didn't."

So Blackie had been in the war, too. Curious, she asked, "Did you get hurt?"

"Yep. Got shot, and nearly got caught."

Frankie blinked, wishing she'd kept quiet.

"I was a paratrooper," Blackie said, wrapping one of her shoes with the tape. "We jumped behind the German lines during the D-Day invasion at Utah Beach —that's in France in a region called Normandy. Got shot before I hit the ground. A buddy dragged me into a hedgerow, then got killed after he tried to help another buddy."

Frankie cringed.

"It was a bloody mess," Blackie said. "Something I'd just as soon forget."

Frankie bit her lip. "I'm sorry."

Blackie sighed. "So am I, kid. A lot of good men died. Just like your father. I was one of the lucky ones. My leg still acts up during the winter." He rubbed his thigh as though it still hurt. "I hid in the hedgerows for three days before our infantry finally drove the Germans out."

He paused, his expression bemused. "Amazing," he said, gazing at her. "I've told you more than I've ever told anyone, including Miss Frazier. Even Sarah. War's ugly."

He took her other shoe and began to work on it. "Your mother must've loved you a lot. Most women who found themselves in the family way without husbands gave up their babies."

"Why?" In spite of Abigale's drinking, Frankie had always felt her mother loved and wanted her. To think other mothers might feel differently was awful.

"Because of the scandal. That would explain why there aren't any pictures of your mom's folks. Once they found out she was expecting a baby, they likely shipped her off to some home for wayward girls. And I got a feeling your dad's folks never knew you existed.

Frankie's stomach lurched and her eyes stung with tears. Studying her tennies, she willed herself not to cry. *If they don't know about me,* she thought, *they'll never believe me and I'll get sent away for sure.* She didn't want to think about what would happen to her if that happened. She stuffed it into the far reaches of her mind. "Hard to say why your mom didn't end up with the Coopers, though," the hobo continued. "But don't worry about it. In another couple of days, we'll find out what happened firsthand."

He handed her the second shoe. "Now put the ranch money in your shoes." When she hesitated, he said, "Look, it's the safest place. If somehow we get split up, at least you'll have enough money to catch a bus home, and to eat. Okay?"

Reluctantly Frankie nodded. The idea of getting split up again was more than she wanted to contemplate. He patted her foot. "Don't worry, we won't get split up. Not if I can help it." *Boy, I hope not,* she thought as she removed the bills from her pocket and put some in each shoe.

The whistle sounded and the freight slowed. "Finally," Blackie said. "Looks like we're pulling off so another train can pass." He gave her a handful of toilet paper. This time, she didn't blush. After the hours cooped up in the car, it was a welcome sight.

When the freight stopped, Blackie picked up the water canteens. "Meet you back here. I'll get some fresh water. Shouldn't be long till we roll again. So make it quick." Frankie nodded and they split up, going in opposite directions.

As Frankie clambered out of the underbrush to return to the train, she was brought up short. A man wearing a red and white bandana tied around his dirty brown hair was urinating in the weeds further down the line of freight cars. His back was toward her.

She gulped. *It can't be. Not again.*

Muskrat!

Armed Man's House

Cop's Home

No Noise

Beware Authorities

CHAPTER 16

Rolled

It was like a recurring nightmare. Frankie felt jinxed. She had to be. Muskrat had appeared out of nowhere four times in the last week! She ducked out of sight and peered through the bushes, looking for Preacher. It wasn't long until he emerged from behind a pine tree, pulling up his pants and chewing on the stub of a cigar. How embarrassing. Frankie rolled her eyes. She could feel herself blushing. He was so dirty. He underwear was as gray and unclean as the rest of him.

Preacher buttoned his pants and ambled over to Muskrat, talking in inaudible tones. Frankie strained to hear. At last Muskrat zipped up his jeans and the two men headed toward the end of the line. She watched them pass several flatcars and then finally climb into a gondola.

Frankie sighed with relief when they sat down, just as she saw Blackie walking back to the freight. *Whee-ew,* she thought. They didn't see him. Blackie climbed into the boxcar and stood in the doorway waiting for her.

Wary, she looked up and down the track. *What if the two tramps reappear?* Her indecision evaporated with the blast of the diesel's whistle. She pushed through the underbrush and sprinted up onto the roadbed. Blackie hauled her aboard. "What took you so long, kid?" he asked.

Should she tell Blackie about seeing the two tramps? Muskrat and Preacher were down the line some twenty cars and there was no way they could get into their boxcar, not with the train beginning to pick up speed. She and Blackie were safe, she figured, so why worry him?

"Took longer than I thought," was all she said.

"Okay. I don't know about you, but I could use some chow. There'll be a crew change in Whitefish. That's a few hours away. In the meantime, let's rustle up something to tide us over." He moved toward the front end where their gear was, and Frankie followed.

While Blackie unrolled his bedroll, Frankie rolled hers up. "Isn't much to choose from," Blackie said, peering at cans of Spam, pork and beans, stew, and a loaf of squashed, stale bread. "Hope you like Spam and pork 'n' beans."

"Sure," she said. "They go together pretty good." It wasn't her favorite, but she wasn't about to complain. She was hungry and grateful to have anything at all to eat.

He opened the can of beans. "Hold this," he said, handing it to Frankie. Some of the liquid sloshed onto her hand when the car bounced. Licking it off, she thought about Havre and her meager fare while waiting for the hobo. *Boy, will I be glad to get off freight trains, sleep in a real bed, and have regular meals,* she thought.

A roller coaster of emotions assailed her. *What would it be like without Blackie?* It was disquieting how dependent she'd become on him. Not just for food, shelter, and protection, but emotionally, too. She'd miss him a lot. When they parted company, would he miss her and their talks as well? She hoped so.

She forced the thought from her mind and watched him pry Spam from the can and slice it on the tin plate. Next, he tore off the end of the loaf of bread. Pressing an indentation, he spooned beans into the space. On top of it, he laid two slices of meat.

"Here," he said, handing Frankie the makeshift sandwich. She giggled. She'd never seen such a messy concoction, or such an appealing one, either.

She took a bite, and sauce from the beans dribbled out the side of her mouth. Blackie laughed when she caught the excess with her tongue. "Mmm," she murmured.

After finishing their meal, they sat cross-legged on the cardboard across from the doorway and watched the forested hillsides scroll by. The sun warmed them. Neither said much.

Later, as the freight slowed and rounded a curve, Frankie thought she saw movement down the line of cars. She leaned forward for a better look, but saw nothing. Blackie hadn't seemed to notice, so she put it out of her mind. Before she knew it, the motion of the train combined with the fresh air and warm sun had lulled her to sleep again.

Her head dropped forward and startled her awake. *Is Blackie dozing?* It looked like it. She rose quietly and, stretched. She moved to the front of the car to get her journal. When the boxcar swayed, she decided against writing in it. It would be too difficult

Maybe I'd better ditch Momma's satchel and put everything in my bedroll, she thought. Then I'll only have one thing to lug around. Quickly she dumped the contents of the satchel into her bedroll, throwing the bag into a corner.

As she started back toward Blackie she stopped.

What's that? she wondered, looking up at the ceiling. *Sounds like footsteps. Is someone on the roof?* Puzzled she moved to the center of the boxcar, listening intently. She heard a grunt and a sound she couldn't identify. Through cracks in the wood ceiling, she could make out two dark shapes.

Frankie screeched when Preacher swung into the boxcar on a rope. He hit Blackie in the chest with his feet.

She gasped. She watched in horror as Blackie pitched backward, his head slamming into the floorboards of the car. Dazed, Blackie sat up and tried to get his bearings, but Preacher was on him in a flash. The two men rolled toward the end of the car, throwing punches.

Before Frankie could move, Muskrat swung down and into the car, too. As he dropped off the end of the rope, the train jolted and swayed. Muskrat lost his balance; he grabbed for the door jamb. The car bucked and his legs slid out into the rushing air. Muskrat clawed wildly at the floorboards, hollering for help.

The car bucked again, this time knocking Frankie off her feet. Muskrat screamed again and then disappeared. Horrified, Frankie stared at the open space. One second Muskrat was there, the next he was gone. Frankie didn't have time to think about Muskrat. She had to help Blackie.

Cautiously, she crawled toward the men now circling one another at the rear of the car.

Her hand brushed the two-by-four. She grabbed it, rose clumsily to her feet and rushed at Preacher, who was cursing and wielding a switchblade. As Frankie swung the board, the car swayed and she fell against Preacher. His knife dropped to the floor. Furious, he wrenched the board out of Frankie's hands and threw her aside. Then he whirled on Blackie.

As the train slowed into an uphill curve, Preacher flung the two-by-four. It glanced off Blackie's head. He staggered, just as the car swayed and pitched him out the doorway.

Frankie screamed.

Preacher spun around, picking up the knife. "Think you can pass yourself off as a boy? Ha! Bull didn't say whether you had to be dead or alive, girlie. A hundred bucks is a hundred bucks." His snake-like eyes gleamed ruthlessly as he lurched toward her, stabbing at her with the knife and trying to grab her arm with the other hand. He got close.

Terrified, Frankie kicked out hard, bringing her foot up between the tramp's legs. Preacher bellowed, clutched his crotch, and rolled toward the rear wall.

Before he could recover, she grabbed their bedrolls and flung them out of the car. For a split second, she hesitated, too frightened to jump off the moving freight. She glanced at Preacher again, held her breath and jumped.

2/10

Crooks in Area

+

Mission Sermon for Food

CHAPTER 17

A Walk

Frankie hit the ground running. When she began to fall, she did what Blackie told her to do. Roll. She crashed through some brush and ended in a heap at the bottom of an embankment. She groaned, spitting out dirt, leaves, and blood. Touching her mouth, she could feel where she'd bitten her lip.

Slowly she raised her head, fearful that Preacher might have followed her. He hadn't! She caught a fleeting glimpse of him doubled over in the doorway of the boxcar just before the train rounded a bend.

Shakily, she got to her feet. Except for her lip, a skinned knee, and several scrapes and bruises, she was okay. If Blackie had fared as well, she'd be happy.

Slightly dizzy, she tried to get her bearings. The freight had disappeared. She had no idea where she was, or where Blackie or their gear might be. The only thing she could do was walk back along the tracks in hopes of finding them.

As she searched, she felt like a bloodhound. She had to be careful, for the terrain at the bottom of the embankment was overgrown with brush. It would be easy to miss things. Just when she was ready to give up, she saw a piece of paper flutter in the breeze. She edged down the embankment and retrieved a photo of Blackie's children. Stuffing it in her jacket pocket, she resumed her search.

A little further along, she spotted their bedrolls. Blackie's had come untied and his belongings were strewn about. Several more photos had come loose from his album and blown into the bushes. She gathered up as many of them she could find and repacked them along with other items in his bedroll, and tied it securely. She shouldered both bedrolls, and crawled up the embankment. She walked along the railroad tracks looking for Blackie. After several minutes without any sign of him she began to feel panicky.

Where is he? Surely she should have found him by now. Maybe he was hurt, unconscious, or she'd missed him. If she didn't find him soon, she'd have to backtrack and look more carefully. She hurried along the embankment calling, "Blackie! Blackie, where are you?"

Finally, she heard a groan. *At last. He's alive! But where is he?* She couldn't see him.

"Blackie!" she called again. Listening carefully, she kept calling until she finally found him at the bottom of a second embankment hidden in a tangle of brush and logs. He had a large knot on his forehead and a bloody gash on his chin.

He tried to smile. "Hi ya, kid," he said. His voice was so faint, Frankie wasn't sure he'd actually spoken.

She squatted beside him. "You okay?"

"Yeah. I guess so. That was too close for comfort." He started to lift his head. "Damn," he swore softly.

"Lie still," Frankie commanded.

She wasn't sure what to do, but she knew they couldn't stay here. She tried to remember what she had read in a first aid book at school. *Check for broken bones. Stop any bleeding.* There'd been something about head injuries, too, but she couldn't remember what it was. First she would take care of the gash on his chin.

Removing her bandana, she studied his injury. *Water.* She needed water, but their canteens were gone, and descending the rugged incline to the Flathead River was impossible. Blackie laughed faintly when she spit on the cloth.

"Hey, I know I got germs," she said, "but it won't kill—" She winced. "Forget I said that." He smiled, and she went to work on his chin.

To her relief, the cut wasn't as bad as it looked, more of a deep scrape.

"Can you stand up?"

"I think so." He raised up on one elbow.

"Here, let me help you." She pulled him into a sitting position. When he leaned against a log, she bit her lip. His face was pale and the knot on his forehead was alarming. "How's your head?" she asked.

"Hurts like hell," he said, touching the bump gingerly.

"Anything else hurt?"

"Yeah, my shoulder." He lifted it slightly, clenching his teeth. "Think I dislocated it. Like once when I got bucked off a horse. Nothing we can do about it now, though."

He looked around. "Let's get moving. Shouldn't be too long till we find a town. I'll have someone look at my head and shoulder then."

Before Blackie could grab his bedroll, Frankie slung it over her back. "It isn't heavy," she lied.

With her help, Blackie got to his feet and they scrambled up to the track. Blackie had to stop often.

Frankie didn't like the way he looked, but she knew they had no choice other than to keep moving.

"Lean on me," Frankie said when they reached the tracks, but Blackie waved her off. She headed up the long curve with Blackie keeping pace, but he kept tripping over the ties. After an hour, Frankie stopped. "We gotta rest." They sat on a knoll in silence for several minutes.

"I could kick myself," Blackie said finally. "Should've known those two would follow us."

Frankie shifted uncomfortably. "It's not your fault, Blackie. I saw them when the train pulled off. That's why I was late getting back. But I didn't think they would bother us because the train was moving. I didn't want to worry you. I should have told you, I guess."

"Yeah," he said. "Well, it's too late now. But next time you see something out of the ordinary, tell me. We don't want any more surprises."

She nodded, shamefaced.

"Where were they anyway?" he asked.

"In a gondola, toward the end of the train."

"Hmm. And there were several flat cars in front of it," Blackie said, as though picturing the makeup of the train in his mind. "They must've seen us sitting in the doorway and crawled over the sill, across the couplers and onto the flat cars. Then up the ladder of the boxcar and across the catwalk, jumping from car to car.

He snorted. "All they needed was a rope to tie to the catwalk, then swing over the edge. Pretty slick plan, but mighty dangerous. You saw what happened to Muskrat."

She shuddered, remembering the tramp's scream as he slid out the door.

"I suppose they planned to roll us. Did Preacher steal anything from you?"

She shook her head. "No. He was after the reward. And he didn't care how he got it." She related Preacher's words about "dead or alive."

"How'd you get away?" Blackie asked.

"I jumped out after I kicked him." She blushed and giggled.

Blackie chuckled, seeming to understand how she'd defended herself. "Where'd you learn that?"

She blushed even redder. "Uh...well...." She rolled her eyes. "I overheard a man at the hotel telling some guy how he'd gotten overly friendly with a lady friend and how she'd let him have it." She giggled again. "It worked. It gave me enough time to grab our stuff and jump. We were lucky the train was slowing on the hill."

"Yep," he agreed. "We might both be standing at the Pearly Gates right now if these tracks didn't need repair and the train had been traveling at its normal speed. Even so, with the car pitching and swaying, I couldn't keep my feet. When I felt myself going, I pushed off and away from the car."

He felt the knot on his forehead again. "Too bad the stuff I landed on wasn't softer. Still, could have been worse."

"Muskrat wasn't so lucky, was he?" Frankie said, feeling slightly queasy. *Had he survived?* She hoped so, but doubted it. She shivered at the thought.

"Afraid not. And if Preacher doesn't watch it, he'll end up under a train one of these days, too."

Struggling to his feet, he said, "So much for depressing subjects. C'mon. We better get moving again. We've got a fair piece to go."

Later, at a deserted siding, they stopped at a leaky water tank for water and a short rest. As they walked on, an eastbound freight passed them. They waved and trudged on.

The sun burned hot in a clear sky. Frankie could feel sweat trickling down the middle of her back under her shirt. She was tired. Dead tired. Her shoulders ached from bruises and the bedrolls, and her skinned knee stung. When would they find a town?

They rounded a bend. Ahead a few hundred yards, a trestle spanned a river. Water sparkled at the bottom of a ravine. When they reached the trestle, Blackie stopped and looked down a craggy embankment. Covered with huckleberry bushes, the steep sides plunged to the river.

Frankie could see that on the other side, the bank flattened out into a broad gravel bar where a man was fishing. The water looked more shallow and not so swift.

Blackie shook his head "I don't like to do this, kid, but it looks like we've got no choice." Grimacing, Blackie limped out onto the trestle.

Frankie didn't much like the idea either. *What if another train comes? But since a train just passed us, that's unlikely. Just? How long has it been?* She was too tired to worry about it now. She sucked in a ragged breath and set off after Blackie.

Slowly, she picked her way across the trestle, one railroad tie at a time. The bedrolls threw her off balance, and the tape had worked loose on one shoe, causing her to trip. She stopped for a moment to catch her breath.

On the other side of the river, the fisherman had been joined by two children and she could see them shouting and waving their arms. She waved back. Their waving became frantic. She squinted, wondering what was wrong.

"Blackie," she yelled, "what's the matter with those people?" Before he could answer, she knew.

It can't be. Not a train! But it was. She looked over her shoulder to see a train rounding the bend into the straightaway toward the trestle. Now its whistle was blaring.

Bad Area

CHAPTER 18

Lucky

"Run, Frankie! Drop the gear!" Blackie yelled.

Frantically he motioned her to run. The hobo was almost across the trestle, some distance ahead of her. The train bore down on her, brakes squealing, metal shrieking against metal. The engineer's whistle screamed in warning blasts.

Struggling with the packs, she managed to leap across several railroad ties before she tripped and fell.

Blackie ran back toward her, gesturing her to drop the bedrolls.

Somehow she had to save her birth certificate, otherwise her grandparent's might not believe she was indeed Frank Cooper's daughter.

She jammed the bedrolls between two ties—they held. She scrambled to her feet and ran for all she was worth.

Up ahead, Blackie was waving her on. A piece of loose tape on her shoe caught on a splinter and she belly-flopped, skidding across the creosote ties. Before she could scramble up, Blackie yanked her to her feet.

"We gotta jump!" Frankie screamed.

Terror swept over Blackie's face as he stared at the engine thundering toward them. He shook his head. "I can't swim!"

Frankie barely caught what he yelled above the clamor of the onrushing freight, but from the look on his face she knew they were in big trouble. They'd die if they didn't jump! She was a good swimmer, but whether she could save Blackie was another matter, especially weighted down with wet clothes. She had read somewhere he might fight her, as drowning people often did. But she would try. No way was she going to lose the closest thing to a father she'd ever had. *No way.*

But Blackie seemed to have a different idea—one to save her. "Love ya, Frankie," he yelled, shoving her towards the edge of the trestle. Realizing what he intended, she grabbed his arm, jerked him off balance and pulled him over the side with her. As they sailed off the trestle into the air, she heard the engine scream past them.

They plummeted toward the water below. Blackie slipped out of Frankie's grasp. Frankie prayed she'd find him, that the river was deep and that there were no rocks. Down she went. Shutting her eyes, she held her breath.

She hit the frigid water with a tremendous splash, then plunged toward the bottom. Her feet touched the rocky riverbed and her lungs felt as if they would explode. She opened her eyes and had only one thought. *Where is Blackie?* Pushing off the bottom, she kicked upward for all she was worth.

Gasping, she popped to the surface like a cork. She began to look for Blackie and grabbed a deep breath.

But, before she could fill her lungs, he grabbed her from behind, pulling her back under. There was no time to be scared, or even think. Instinctively she slammed her elbow into his chest. Air whooshed out of him and he clawed for the surface. She came up and grabbed his hair to tow him in. He thrashed his way out of her grip.

"No," she gasped, choking on a mouthful of water. In desperation, she tried to grab him again but missed. When all seemed lost she heard, "I got him, son." A big, hairy arm looped over Blackie's shoulder and across his chest. To her relief she recognized the fisherman they'd seen from the trestle. Blackie flailed around, then seemed to lose consciousness.

"Can you make it?" the man called.

Dully, she nodded and swam after him as he towed Blackie in. The fisherman hauled Blackie up onto the gravel bar, flipped him onto his stomach and began rhythmically putting pressure on his upper back. Frankie realized the freight had stopped. It had backed up, and one of the engineers jumped off and joined the two children on the river bank.

"We could have killed you!" he shouted, shaking his fist.

Frankie stared at him blankly. *If only you knew,* she thought. She felt sick to her stomach and disoriented. Her legs buckled. She sank to her knees beside Blackie, and she began to cry.

Coughing up water and gasping for air, Blackie rolled over and pulled her into his arms. "It's okay,

Frankie," he said, hugging her. "It's okay. We made it."

She nodded, but couldn't stop crying. She buried her head in the crook of his neck and sobbed. When she finally realized that they were safe, she began to hiccup and giggle hysterically. Between giggles, hiccups, and tears, she finally ran down. With a sniff, she swiped at her eyes and nose with her wet wrist.

"Oh, Blackie, I'm sorry. I just...."

"It's okay, Frankie." He gave her a shaky smile. "I should have known better. It's my fault and if you hadn't pulled me off, we'd've been killed."

His eyes glistened with tears. For a moment, Frankie thought he might cry. Then he sucked in a deep breath and exhaled slowly.

"Losing Sarah and the kids was horrible. Losing you would have been too much." He shook his head. "Never in all the years I've been on the rails, have I had so many close calls."

Frankie bit her lip. "Maybe I'm jinxed."

He laughed lightly and his eyes seemed to twinkle a little "Could be, but I doubt it. Just a bad combination of wrong time, wrong place." He sighed. "Maybe someone's trying to tell us something."

"Someone?"

"Well, like maybe our guardian angel."

Slowly he got to his feet and turned to the engineer. "Sorry to pull that stunt on you, but we had some trouble with a coupla tramps. Sure would appreciate it if we could hitch a ride into Whitefish."

He winced, lifting his shoulder slightly. "Dislocated my shoulder, too." He briefly related their run-in with Muskrat and Preacher.

The engineer scratched his chin. After his initial outburst, he seemed embarrassed. "Jack oughta have room in the caboose." He nodded toward the freight. Frankie could see the conductor watching them from the rear platform of the caboose.

Blackie turned to the fisherman who'd pulled him out of the river. "Much obliged. Don't know what we'd've done without you, mister."

The fisherman chuckled, pulling on a pair of jeans over wet boxer shorts. "Glad I could help. Ain't every day I pull a fish outta this river as big as you."

Blackie and Frankie followed the engineer back to the freight. He returned their bedrolls and as they walked he instructed them to stay put in the caboose. Soon the freight rumbled on its way. A conductor appeared. Lighting his pipe, he squinted at Blackie through a cloud of pleasant-smelling smoke. "You're one lucky man. If the kid hadn't pulled you off the trestle, well..." Quickly he changed subjects. "I imagine you could use some coffee. And probably a shot of whiskey, too."

"I'll pass on the whiskey." Blackie said. "I never drink on the road. In fact, I don't drink much at all. Caused too much trouble in the past."

He smiled at Frankie. "Besides, I gotta get this young fella home in one piece. Don't need any more complications. Some coffee would hit the spot, though."

Frankie returned his smile. Relief washed over her. The conductor nodded and moved to the rear of the car to pour two mugs of coffee.

Then a horrible thought struck her. "What if we run into Preacher again?" she exclaimed, her stomach fluttering.

Blackie shook his head. "Not gonna happen. Once I get my shoulder and head looked at, we're riding the cushions." He took a sip from the steaming mug the conductor handed him.

"Cushions?" She stared at him.

He laughed. "Cushions. Seats. We don't need to risk running into Preacher. We've got enough cash to get us the rest of the way home on a passenger train. I'll find a job, work a couple of weeks, then head north in time for fishing season."

Us? Home? Was it a slip of the tongue? Do I dare hope he might settle near my grandparents, let alone hope they will accept me?

Then she remembered something else. Had Blackie really said he loved her before she pulled him off the trestle? Or was that a figment of her imagination?

Bad Water

Caution

157

CHAPTER 19

The Doctor

Late that afternoon the freight rumbled over a trestle into the lakeside mountain town of Whitefish, Montana. They pulled onto a siding, clanking to a stop. Frankie tagged along with Blackie as he thanked the crew for bringing them into town.

As they left the yard, the engineer leaned out of his cab and shouted, "Doc McDowell's office is across from the hospital on Park. He'll fix you up. He swaps services for work, too."

"Thanks," Blackie called. He waved and set off toward town. Frankie kept step alongside him.

They found the doctor's office in a two-story wooden building. The office had just closed when they arrived, but the heavy-set, balding doctor could see Blackie needed attention. He motioned Blackie to follow him. To Frankie he said, "Why don't you sit in the waiting room while I examine your friend?"

Huh? Why can't I tag along? Blackie is only going to have his head and shoulder treated. I don't want to let Blackie out of my sight. I know it's silly, but I don't want to lose him. Not again.

When she frowned, Blackie said, "It's okay, Doc, he's my kid."

His kid? If pigs could fly! More than anything else in the world, she wished she were Blackie's kid. But she wasn't, and no amount of wishing could change the fact. The doctor shrugged, motioning Frankie to follow them.

Frankie followed down the hallway, wondering what would happen once they got to Tonasket. *Blackie won't just take off for Alaska as soon as we get there, will he? He'll stick around to make sure Grandma and Grandpa accept me? Cripes, what if they don't, then what? Will Blackie let me go with him?* It was all so unsettling. Her eyes stung as she entered the examination room.

While the doctor checked Blackie's head and shoulders, Frankie stood in a corner and watched. "That's a nasty bump you've got," the doctor said, "but you'll be all right. If you feel dizzy or sick to your stomach, I want to see you pronto! Otherwise, you can leave tomorrow." He ran his hands quickly over the hobo's back and shoulders, then before Frankie realized what was happening, he wrenched Blackie's dislocated shoulder back into place. Blackie yelped and turned pale.

Frankie flinched. "Don't hurt my...." *My what?* she thought, swallowing the rest. *Father?* There she went again, wishing for the impossible.

"It's okay, Frankie." Blackie blinked, his eyes were teary. "I'd forgotten how much that hurts. Whoo-wee!"

The doctor smiled sympathetically. "Sorry. I hate to do that, but it's easier when you don't expect it. Want a sling?"

Blackie shook his head. "Nah, I'll be okay. What do I owe you, Doc?"

The doctor shrugged. "If your kid's up to spading my wife's garden and pulling some weeds in the morning, we'll call it square. I don't want you doing anything heavy, though." He gave Blackie a pointed glance as though knowing he would do more than watch Frankie work.

"Okay, Doc, I hear you."

Nephew? Kid? Frankie bit her lip to keep from saying, *How about daughter, for a change?* She glanced at Blackie, wondering what he thought of the doctor's remark about his "kid."

If he noticed, he didn't let on. Blackie was getting directions to the man's house. *Doesn't he care? If only he'd stick around. If, if, if.* She wished it didn't make any difference. But it did.

The doctor said, "I'll tell my wife to expect you in the morning then. And remember, any problems with that head, you know where I am."

"Gosh," Frankie said, as they walked away from the doctor's office. "Why didn't he charge something?"

"You prob'ly didn't notice. There's a hobo sign scratched into one of the boards by his door."

"Oh? What'd it look like?"

"A plus sign and a head with a hat. Means 'good doctor, free. During the Depression, when there wasn't much work, the doctor probably didn't charge anything.

160

Even now, if he has something he needs done, he'll let a 'bo pay for his services that way. Like digging up his wife's garden."

It sounded like a good system, but now she was anxious to get home. "When are we leaving?" Frankie asked.

"Tomorrow. We'll catch the evening train. That way we'll be sure to get McDowell's garden done before we head out."

He stopped to roll a cigarette. "I could use some chow. Afterwards, we'll go to a secluded spot I know down by the river. We won't be bothered there. Hungry?"

Frankie nodded. Until he'd mentioned it, she hadn't realized she was starved. He led the way to a mom-and-pop diner not far from the train depot. The food was hearty and they stuffed themselves with roast beef, mashed potatoes, carrots, and bread pudding.

After supper they walked to the Whitefish River. They found a wooded area where Blackie felt they would be safe. Spreading their bedrolls on the ground, they settled down under the trees.

Soon Blackie was snoring, but Frankie had trouble falling asleep. Tossing and turning, she worried about the future, afraid her grandparents wouldn't want her and Blackie would leave her behind.

Morning came and they gathered up their things. Heavy-hearted, Frankie trudged behind Blackie as they set off for town.

After breakfast Blackie bought her a pair of shoes to replace her worn-out tennies.

"You're awful quiet today," he said. "Why so glum?" Frankie just shrugged, and he peered at her searchingly.

Doc McDowell's place was on the outskirts of town, a large single-story red-brick house surrounded by a white picket fence, fruit trees, and flower beds. As they came through the rear gate, Blackie pointed at a hobo sign carved into it.

"This means 'work, food.'" He ran his finger over another sign. "This one means 'nice lady.'"

A plump, grey-haired woman with a pleasant face answered their knock. Mrs. McDowell obviously enjoyed her cooking as much as her husband did. Taking them out to a spot behind the shed, she gave Frankie a spade. While Frankie dug up the garden, Blackie pulled weeds with his uninjured arm. By the time they finished in mid-afternoon, they were both dirty and drenched with sweat.

Surveying the garden and the neat piles of weeds, Mrs. McDowell smiled approvingly. "My husband said you'd do a good job, and he was right. It's been a long time since I've had a 'bo do any work for me."

Pointing toward the woodshed, she said, "During the Depression, I had hobos chop wood or do other chores. Now it seems the only time we see a 'bo is when Earl treats one for something or other."

She waved them toward the house. "I'll put on a pot of coffee while you wash up. I'm sure you must be hungry."

They followed her across the lawn and through the back door into a large cozy kitchen full of mouth-watering smells. "The bathroom's that way," Mrs. McDowell said, pointing to a hallway off the kitchen.

Frankie washed quickly and helped set the table while Blackie cleaned up. The woman watched her intently. Did the woman sense she was really a girl? For one thing, her hair was beginning to grow out a little.

While they ate vegetable soup and thick roast beef sandwiches, Mrs. McDowell asked Blackie how he had gotten injured and what had brought them to Whitefish. After hearing their hair-raising story, she walked with them to the gate.

Laughing softly, she glanced at Frankie. "Earl thought you might be a girl. Either that or the prettiest 'boy' he'd ever seen."

She chuckled, then became serious. "I'm sorry about your mother, dear." Putting her arm around Frankie's shoulder, she said, "Good luck with your grandparents. I wish all my grandchildren were as sweet-natured and helpful as you," she added.

"Thank you, ma'am," Frankie said. "And thank you for lunch, and this." She held up the bag of sandwiches,

163

cookies, and apples Mrs. McDowell had given them for the train ride.

The doctor's wife smiled affectionately. "You're welcome, my dear. Come see me if you're ever back in Whitefish."

She patted Blackie's arm. "That goes for you, too, Clarence. But I don't imagine we'll see you for a while. At least, not if you find that place you've been hankering for."

"No, ma'am," Blackie replied. "With a little luck, I'll find the right place."

Near Tonasket, Frankie wanted to say, but didn't. She swallowed the lump in her throat.

After waving good-bye to Mrs. McDowell, Frankie followed Blackie across town to the train depot. As they walked, he gave her a brief history of hoboing.

"What we did today, thousands of 'bos did during the Depression," he said. "There used to be women like the doctor's wife all over the country. Lots of 'em didn't have it much better than the 'bos did."

"Only difference was, the women had a roof over their heads. Usually, they had a garden and some fruit trees. With a few chickens for eggs, a cow for milk, maybe a calf or pig for meat, most of 'em got along. And in those days, anyone lucky enough to have something generally shared it. Of course, there were always some that wouldn't."

"Why wouldn't people share if someone was hungry?"

"Greed? Afraid they'd run out of food? Who knows. Remember one of my cousins bringing home a hitchhiker. I couldn't have been more than nine or ten at the time. This kid was out of Chicago, name of Rollins."

He stopped to roll a cigarette. "Well, my aunt liked Rollins, so he stayed. For four years. He told us stories about the bread lines he'd stood in during the dead of winter. There were lines of men, three and four wide for more than a block, waiting for a bowl of cabbage soup and a slice of stale bread. When a guy'd eaten, he'd go back to the end of the line and wait his turn again."

Frankie shivered. It sounded awful. No matter how bad things had been, she and Abigale had always managed to have something to eat.

Curious, she asked, "Where'd they sleep?"

"In hobo jungles, mostly. Sometimes under bridges and trestles. Jails. Or in places like the missions run by churches. Rollins said he once slept with over two hundred other men at the Salvation Army during a blizzard. They were the lucky ones. The ones who weren't so lucky froze to death trying to sleep in doorways or empty boxcars."

Frankie tried to imagine it. She couldn't. Blackie continued, "The jungles were bigger than they are now, too. Some had as many as a hundred shanties in 'em. Wasn't uncommon for bulls to burn them to the ground."

He sighed. "'Course, once the war started, things got better. For some people, anyway."

Shortly after Blackie bought their tickets, they boarded the westbound train. They found their seats and stowed their gear in the overhead bins. As soon as the train got under way Frankie fell asleep.

Hours later she was awakened by early morning light streaming through the window. Across from her Blackie snored softly. She yawned and stretched. The muscles in her arms ached and the blisters on her fingers burned from the spading work.

She crept past sleeping passengers to the lavatory. Splashing water on her face, she was glad to see her black eye had faded. She smiled at her reflection. But her reflection revealed something new and unfamiliar too. The shirt Blackie had gotten for her at the Sally was getting tight. Her chest was beginning to fill out. So much had happened in the last few weeks she hadn't noticed before. No wonder Ellie Mae had guessed she was a girl. It would be nice to be a girl again.

She cocked her head to one side, studying herself in the mirror. The short hair was kind of cute. She'd never had short hair before. Maybe she'd keep it this way.

As she returned to her seat, the conductor called out, "Next stop, Wenatchee!"

Blackie yawned. "We get off here, then catch the local up the valley." He stood up and stretched, then ambled off toward the restrooms. "Back in a minute."

While he was gone, Frankie worried about what would happen once they reached Tonasket. The "what ifs" were never-ending. By the time the hobo returned, she had worked herself into a dither. At the Wenatchee depot, they boarded the Okanogan Valley passenger train. Frankie was still fretting.

Pulling out of Wenatchee, Frankie saw hobo jungles scattered along the banks of the Columbia River. As their train passed a string of freight cars, Frankie jerked upright. Standing in the doorway of a boxcar, with a gunny sack at his feet, was Preacher, smoking a cigar. When would they get rid of the tramp? He was like an evil phantom. Frankie scrunched down in her seat.

"What's the matter?" Blackie asked.

Frankie pointed, not looking up.

"Him again," Blackie said, not seeming overly surprised. "Frankie, that freight's bound west toward Seattle. You're safe. He won't get you. Couple, three hours and you'll be home."

Sure, she thought, sighing dejectedly. *Then what?*

As the train chugged around a bend, the view from the window captured her attention. It was breathtaking. The fruit trees were in full bloom. Mile after mile of blossoming orchards stretched up the slopes from the Columbia. The valley was a magic place, awash with delicate color. Frankie felt she was riding through a pink and white cloud. She remembered the pictures of her mother and father under the apple trees. "I wish

Momma was here to see this," she murmured. "It's beautiful."

Blackie leaned over to look out the window. "It sure is. I'd forgotten just how beautiful the orchards are this time of year. Maybe someday one of 'em will be mine."

Does that mean you might settle in the valley? She wanted to ask, but was afraid to. Instead she said, "Are they all apple trees?"

He shook his head. "Most are, but there are pear, peach, apricot, and cherry trees, too. Not sure just which is which. Your grandparents will be able to tell you, though."

Frankie bit her lip. She wished he hadn't reminded her about her grandparents. The what-ifs came thundering back. Dejected, she turned and watched the countryside.

By the time the train pulled into Tonasket, Frankie was ready to run. There was no way her grandparents would want her. Not a bastard. They'd be too embarrassed to claim her as their own. She wished she hadn't come. She sat glued to her seat.

"C'mon, Frankie," Blackie said softly, pulling their bedrolls down from the rack. Obediently, she got to her feet. Tears teetered on the edge of her lashes before spilling down her cheeks.

"Don't cry, Frankie," the hobo said, gently hugging her. "There's nothing to be afraid of. Your grandparents aren't going to run you off. You'll see." She hoped he was right. Plagued with uncertainty, she followed him off the train. Tonasket wasn't very big, just a short main street lined with stores and surrounded by houses clustered along the Okanagan River. Frankie could see more houses on a ridge, and a sawmill's smokestack. The town was surrounded by a breathtaking pallet of pink and white blossoms. She liked the town and hoped she'd get to live here. If only....

"Nothing left of the lunch Mrs. McDowell gave us," Blackie said, interrupting her thoughts. He tossed the bag into a trash barrel on the station platform. "We'll grab some chow, then find your grandparents' place, okay?"

Looking at her shoes, Frankie nodded. Blackie stopped and put his hand gently on her shoulder. "Frankie, you shouldn't work yourself into such a lather. It's going to be okay." He lifted her chin. "Really it is."

She looked up into the blue eyes of the man she wished, with all her heart, could be her dad and forced a smile. *Why can't I tell him how I feel?* she wondered.

"That's better. Now, let's go eat. Okay? Good."

In a small cafe, Frankie picked at her food, thinking of the rejection she was sure she faced. Her stomach clenched.

"Looking for the Cooper place," Blackie said to the waitress, as he was paying the bill.

"There are several Coopers hereabouts," the middle-aged waitress replied. "Most likely you're looking for John Cooper. The others are his kids. Nice folks. All of 'em." She looked Blackie and Frankie over. "If you're looking for work, John's looking for someone to build a full-fledged bathhouse, with toilets and showers for his pickers."

"Good people to work for?" Blackie said.

"The best!"

Blackie shot Frankie a reassuring look. She shrugged. Maybe it wouldn't be as bad as she imagined.

After Blackie thanked the waitress and got directions to the Cooper orchard, they walked through town and across a bridge. Smoke rose through trees close to where a creek spilled into the Okanagan River. Another hobo jungle? A few hundred yards north of the bridge, a road wound up through orchards.

"This looks like your grandparents' place," Blackie said, pointing toward a house atop a knoll. It was a two-story, blue-trimmed white house, with a large front porch and a swing. The house was encircled by apple trees.

Frankie stopped in the middle of the road to gaze at the house. *Home?* There was something inviting about it. She looked back across the river toward the small town. She was even more certain she wanted to live here. Now if only her grandparents would let her.

As they started up the driveway, Blackie chuckled. "We're in luck, Frankie," he said pointing to a carving on the Coopers' mailbox post. It was of a smiling cat.

"What's it mean?"

"Good woman lives here—will give food for work."

"Really?"

"Yep. Imagine your grandparents hired hobos to prune, thin and pick apples. With a new bathhouse, they'll have more help than they can handle. Bathhouses are few and far between. Most orchards just have an outhouse and the river to bathe in." He smiled gently at Frankie. "Let's go find your grandma."

Still uncertain, Frankie followed Blackie up to the house and onto the porch. She held her breath as he knocked on the door.

He waited a minute or two, then turned to her. "We may have to go 'round back."

Just then the door opened. A pretty blonde woman, wearing dark blue slacks and a white blouse, smiled at him. "May I help you?" she asked.

She looked at the bedroll slung over Blackie's shoulder. "Oh, you must be here about the bathhouse. Dad's at the mill." She glanced at Frankie. Her eyes widened in disbelief.

Behind the young woman, Frankie saw a plump woman with curly red-and-gray hair coming down the hall toward them, wiping her hands on an apron.

"Who is it, Anna?" the woman asked.

"It's Frankie, Mother," the young woman replied. Tears welled up in her hazel eyes. "Frankie's come home."

CHAPTER 20

A Reunion

"Frankie?" Mrs. Cooper walked through the living room toward the door. "You must be mistaken, Anna. Frank's... The rest trailed off as she stopped and stared at Frankie. She grabbed the back of an overstuffed chair to steady herself and gasped. "It can't be!" The color drained from her face, and she slipped to the floor.

Anna dropped to her knees, patting her mother's cheeks, tears streaming down her cheeks. "Momma, Momma." she cried.

"Get a wet washcloth, Frankie," Blackie said. "The bathroom should down there somewhere." He pointed toward the door Mrs. Cooper had come through.

Frankie raced off, hoping she hadn't caused her grandmother to have a stroke or a heart attack. She tore through a fragrant kitchen and beyond, in the bathroom, she found the cloth she needed, ran it under a faucet and dashed back to her grandmother.

Blackie had carried the woman to a rose colored brocade sofa. Anna was crouched beside her, patting her mother's hand and sniffling.

Blackie took the wet cloth from Frankie and laid it across the older woman's forehead. Mrs. Cooper's eyes flickered and slowly opened.

Her eyes are green like mine, Frankie marveled. *And I kind of look like her.* A warm feeling washed over

Frankie. It quickly evaporated. *What if she doesn't accept me?* The woman's eyes settled on Frankie. In a choked voice she said, "This isn't funny, young man! How dare you impersonate my son? Tears pooled in her eyes. Frankie's dead! Who...who are you?"

Frankie saw confusion and anger in her grandmother's eyes and, for a moment, wished she hadn't come. But she had come too far to quit now. She had to convince this woman that she was indeed Frank Cooper's daughter.

"Ma'am," Blackie said. "I'm sorry we upset you, but Frankie's your granddaughter."

"What?" The woman struggled to sit up. He quickly tried to assist her. She shook Blackie off. "Granddaughter? This boy? That's nonsense! Frank never married. And if you think I'll believe this boy is Frank's son you're crazy."

"Moth...er," Anna stammered. She peered a Frankie for a long moment. "He's...she's a girl. Look at her, mother. No boy has a face that pretty! And, he's...she's the spitting image of Frank." She pointed to a tinted photograph, proudly displayed on an upright piano, of Frank Cooper in a Royal Canadian Air Force dress uniform. "Mother, see the likeness?"

Mrs. Cooper's eyes darted uncertainly from the photograph to Frankie. When her mother didn't look convinced, Anna took a different tack, and Frankie had the feeling she was going to like her aunt a lot. "She's got the same curly red hair, Mom." She laughed softly.

173

"Just like yours and Frank's. And the green eyes. Plus all his freckles."

Mrs. Cooper, looking bewildered, stared at Frankie. Frankie sensed her grandmother was wavering. *Would my birth certificate convince my grandmother?* "I've got my birth certificate," Frankie volunteered, heading toward the front door where she'd dropped her bedroll.

"Oh my, oh my," Mrs. Cooper said, her eyes glistening with tears.

While Frankie untied her bedroll on the living room rug, Blackie crouched beside her. He said, "Frankie, show them your dad's book." Under his breath so that the others wouldn't hear he added, "You're doing just fine, Frankie. The book and birth certificate will convince her."

Frankie looked at him bleakly. *What if they don't convince my grandmother?*

"What book?" Mrs. Cooper asked, her voice squeaky.

Frankie pulled it from her bedroll. "Rudyard Kipling."

"Kim?" the woman said, fresh tears forming in her eyes. "The book I gave Frank for his birthday?"

"Yes, ma'am," Frankie replied, and handed it to her.

With trembling hands, Mrs. Cooper opened the book to the inscription she had written so long ago. She wiped her tears away with the washcloth.

"Where did you get this? Who gave it to you?" she asked with an expression that was somewhere between confusion and suspicion.

"Well...." Frankie stammered, feeling uncomfortable. Why wouldn't her grandmother believe her? She hadn't stolen the book. She sucked in a breath and let it out slowly. "I found it in my mother's things after she died.... Momma never told me much about Dad, or about any of you. I only found out about him from these." She quickly took the bundle of her father's letters and photographs from her bedroll and held them out to her grandmother.

The woman looked from Frankie to the packet of papers, as if trying to decide whether or not to take hold of a red-hot poker. Finally, she took them. Silently, she read the letters her son had so lovingly written to Abigale. No one in the room moved or spoke. Finally Blackie cleared his throat and moved over to put an arm around Frankie. She leaned against him, trembling.

She has to believe me. She just has to! Frankie cried silently to herself. *All this can't have been for nothing.*

Frankie held her breath as Mrs. Cooper finished reading the letters and looked through the photographs and news clippings. She then unfolded the last piece of paper, Frankie's birth certificate.

"Frances Jane. What a lovely name. Ohhh," the woman cried, dabbing her eyes with the washcloth. "It's true, isn't it? You really are Frank's child."

"Yes, ma'am." Frankie sighed, relieved that Mrs. Cooper at last believed her. But would she let her stay? Now Frankie wished she and Blackie were on the rails headed somewhere, anywhere. She didn't want to be told to "git." She blinked back tears, stomach fluttering, hoping against hope she wouldn't be turned away.

"You said your mother died, child?" Mrs. Cooper said. "How did you find us? Why didn't you come sooner? And who is this man?" She nodded toward Blackie. "My goodness, this is all so unbelievable. Anna, make some coffee. I can't imagine what I'm going to tell your father...."

Later, at the kitchen table, Mrs. Cooper stirred her coffee aimlessly as she listened to Frankie's story. In front of her lay her son's letters, the photographs, and the Kipling book. Frankie sat next to her.

Blackie helped Anna put away the fresh-baked cinnamon rolls and loaves of golden-brown bread she and her mother had made earlier that day.

"We knew Frank was smitten with your mother," Mrs. Cooper said, smiling at Frankie. "Abigale was a sweet girl. But Mrs. Ross—that's Abigale's mother— was fit to be tied when her daughter took up with a Catholic."

She gazed out the kitchen window, as though looking off to another time. "The Rosses were Fundamentalists —Holy Rollers—and Mr. Ross was a minister, to boot. They couldn't bear the thought of their daughter dating Frank, a Catholic, much less marrying him. And having a child out of wedlock—well, I can imagine what they thought of that!"

Frankie looked down at her hands, flushing, feeling again the humiliation her mother must have felt.

"I'm so sorry about your mother. She was a dear girl. I often wondered what became of her after her parents moved back to Kentucky. I just wish she would have brought you home. We would have taken care of you both." She dabbed her eyes with a tissue. "In those days, girls in your mother's circumstance didn't keep their babies." Her lips smiled, but her eyes were sad. "It took a lot of courage for your mother to keep you, my dear. Few girls would have, much less could have. Your grandfather and I can't undo the past, but we can give you a home now."

"You...you mean, I can stay?" Frankie blurted.

Mrs. Cooper laughed. "Of course you can, child. Did you think we'd turn you away?" She paused and studied Frankie's bleak face. "You did, didn't you? Oh my goodness, Frances, did you think just because your parents weren't married, we'd..."

Tears stung Frankie's eyes. "I didn't know. Everything's been so crazy since Momma died. I didn't know if I'd ever find you, or if you'd want me if I did."

"For goodness sakes. Of course we want you. Believe me, you'll always have a home with us."

Frankie's lower lip began to tremble as relief rushed through her. *I get to stay, Momma,* she cried silently.

Now she had a home. A real home. Then the tragedy of her mother's death hit her full force and she began to cry.

Alarmed, Blackie pulled a handkerchief from his pant pocket. Before he could move toward her, Mrs. Cooper gathered Frankie in her arms, quietly shushing her. Blackie smiled, his face gentle and caring.

After a while, Frankie sniffed and swiped at her eyes. Her grandmother handed her a tissue. Frankie blew her nose.

"Now, I'm sure your grandfather would like to get acquainted with you," Mrs. Cooper said. "Anna, why don't you take this nice young man over to the mill and get your dad. He's probably down at the pond. I'll show Frances her room."

Anna smiled at Blackie. "If you're looking for a job, Mr. Black, Dad's always...."

"Clarence. Please, call me Clarence."

"Um, yes..." she murmured, flushing slightly. "Well, if you're looking for a job, Clarence, Dad's always looking for good men at the mill. Or you could frame the bathhouse Dad's having built for our pickers."

Clarence? Frankie thought. *Not Blackie?* Her gaze shifted from the hobo to her aunt. Now Blackie was smiling at Anna. *Criminy,* Frankie thought, *I think Blackie likes her.* And from the expression on her aunt's face, Frankie was sure Anna felt the same way.

"Mill work's more up my alley," Blackie said.

As he ushered Anna out the back door, Frankie heard Blackie ask, "Do you work?"

"Not yet. I got my teaching certificate a couple weeks ago from Bellingham Teacher's College, but there aren't any primary jobs open till fall. I'll help Dad thin apples and then find a waitress job or something until a teaching position opens up this fall."

After the door shut, Mrs. Cooper said, "Blackie seems like a nice young man. Tell me about him."

As they toured the large house, Frankie told her what she knew about Blackie. She finished up with, "And he's thinking about buying an orchard when he gets through fishing in Alaska."

Her grandmother smiled, approvingly. "Maybe around here?"

"Uh-huh," Frankie said, "I'd like that a lot. He's nice, real nice." Frankie's face beamed with affection. "If Blackie hadn't helped me, I'd never have made it home. I almost got killed—more than once—and he was there every time to save me. Riding the rails was dangerous—real dangerous."

Mrs. Cooper nodded. She wrapped her arm around Frankie's shoulder as they moved along the upstairs hall. "I think that you should have Fra...your father's room."

It was a large, well-furnished room, larger than any Frankie had ever called her own. The window overlooked the orchard, and to her delight, her father's model airplanes still hung from the ceiling.

"You'll probably want to take down your dad's model airplanes and put up girl things. I never had the heart to take them down.... He had such a love for flying. Before the war, he flew with a neighbor every chance he got. Soon as Frank heard Canada was taking our boys, he was off to join up."

Frankie surveyed the collection of balsa wood planes and the airplane posters covering the walls. There was a closeness to her father in this room, something she'd never had and wanted to keep. "No, I'd like to leave it the way it is. I like it."

"Well, whatever you want is fine with me. This is your room now, Frances." Mrs. Cooper smiled at her and then turned away to smooth the patchwork quilt on one of the twin beds.

"Um…It's Frankie, actually."

"I'm sorry, what was that?" Mrs. Cooper asked looking up from her task.

Frankie cleared her throat. "Well, it's just…" she sighed. "I probably should have said something earlier, but nobody ever calls me 'Frances.' My name has always been 'Frankie.' The only time Momma ever called me Frances Jane was when she was mad at me." Frankie's voice trailed off as she tried to blot out the image of her mother the night she died. Tears welled and she fought to keep them at bay. "So please just call me Frankie, okay?" she finished with her eyes turned to the floor.

"Oh, I thought you took the name 'Frankie' because you were pretending to be a boy. I didn't realize... Well, that's what we always called..." Mrs. Cooper shook her head with a bemused smile on her lips. "Child, you are your father's daughter, right down to your nickname. And yes, I'll call you Frankie if you'll call me Grandma."

Frankie grinned, and Grandma put her arm around her and led her into the hall. "Come on, let's get some fresh sheets for your bed."

Good Doctor, Free

Sick Care

Work/Food

Good Route

Best Way

Nice Lady

181

CHAPTER 21

A New Beginning

The next couple of weeks were a whirlwind of questions, school and visitors. The Coopers, it seemed, were popular folks. There was always someone stopping by—aunts, uncles, friends, neighbors, church members. With each new visitor, Frankie's story had to be told again, which at first made her uneasy. Her grandmother, though, skillfully deflected potentially embarrassing questions, and Frankie's fears subsided. She reveled in having so many people to call family, even if keeping them all straight was a bit overwhelming.

Her grandfather hired Blackie on at the mill, culling lumber. He slept in a picker's cabin and ate his meals with the Cooper family.

The day after Frankie arrived and went back to school, she had written to Mrs. O'Reilly and Miss Frazier. To her delight, she soon received a reply from Mrs. O'Reilly.

According to the cook, Ziggy had repaired and cleaned up the hotel, and things were definitely changing for the better. One thing hadn't changed, though. The old codgers were still playing cards and telling outlandish stories.

"They're tickled you're safe with your family and they send their love. You'll be interested to hear," Mrs. O'Reilly continued, "that Helen Spalding had a warrant sworn out on Charlie. Seems he stole the funeral parlor funds, so she's put the business up for sale and is moving back to Fargo. I could've told her he was a scoundrel."

Mrs. O'Reilly had saved the best news for last. "You know that story you wrote? Well, your teacher went ahead and entered it in a newspaper contest even though you aren't living here anymore. Your story took second place. Personally, I think it should've taken first, as the winning story wasn't anything much, but we're all real proud just the same."

Frankie's grandparents arranged to have Abigale's body returned to Tonasket to be buried alongside their son's. The headstone Frankie had worked so hard for was shipped to the town cemetery as well.

"I don't care what anybody might think," her grandmother had said firmly. "As far as John and I are concerned, Frank and Abigale belong together and deserve to rest in peace just like any married couple." Frankie had never loved anyone as much as she loved her grandma at that moment.

For a long time, Frankie thought Blackie might not leave after all, but one night the dreaded moment came when the family was playing Monopoly at the kitchen table. Frankie had helped Anna make popcorn and hot chocolate for everyone.

Blackie drank the last of his cocoa. "The past two weeks have been the nicest I've spent in a long time." He looked first at the Coopers and then at Frankie. Her heart sank. "But we all know everything comes to an end." He set his empty mug on the table. "I'm catching out tonight. Signed on with a troller for the season. I'll be sailing to Alaska first of next week."

Frankie's eyes pricked with tears. Though she knew Blackie would leave sometime, he hadn't mentioned coming back. *Should I ask him? What if he says no? What if...* She stole a glance across the table at her aunt. *I wish I knew what Anna is thinking.* Anna stared without expression into her cup.

Doesn't Anna want him to come back? For several nights, Frankie had drifted off to sleep hearing the murmur of Blackie and Anna's voices as they talked on the porch swing beneath her window. *Doesn't that mean they like each other? And surely on one of the walks they have taken together, Blackie must have told Anna about his plan to someday own an orchard? There are hundreds of orchards around Tonasket.*

"No chance of getting you to change your mind?" her grandfather asked. Blackie shook his head. "Well, son, I'm sorry to see you go, and that's a fact." He slid back his chair. "We can at least walk you to the yard."

Off in the distance, Frankie heard a train's whistle. As the family walked down the hill to the railroad tracks, Blackie and Anna walked side by side, talking quietly. Maybe they didn't like each other as much as Frankie had thought. It was all so confusing. All Frankie wanted was for Blackie to come back, and soon.

A steam engine rumbled, its motor idling as they crossed the tracks. They walked with Blackie to a siding where flat cars loaded with lumber and refrigerator cars filled with apples waited. Blackie walked along the track until he found an empty. He tossed his bedroll into the car, and stood there for a long moment, looking at Frankie. "Gonna miss you, Frankie."

Over her head, he smiled at her grandparents and Anna. Frankie couldn't see if her aunt returned his smile.

It's now or never, Frankie thought. "Are you coming back?" she barked, her voice more angry than she intended.

Blackie blinked as though surprised by her boldness. Then he chuckled. "Between working and spending time with your aunt and not wanting to horn in on your time with your new grandparents, I've neglected you. I'm sorry." He wrapped an arm around her and pulled her along at a fast trot as the locomotive gave two short warning blasts and jolted forward. Above the rattle of the freight, he shouted, "I'll be back, Frankie! I'll be back mid-October. Then you and your aunt can help me find an orchard."

Her doubts must have shown on her face. "Believe me, Frankie. I'll come home. Really, I will!" He paused momentarily, his voice catching. "I gotta, 'cause I love you." His lips brushed her forehead and then he swung up into the car as the freight began to pick up speed. Standing in the the doorway, he gave her a smile that told Frankie that he really did love her.

"I love you, too, Blackie," she yelled back, waving and crying. She watched the train until the last flicker of rear markers faded into the darkness. Tears still trickled down her cheeks as she walked back to her grandparents and aunt. Anna was dabbing her eyes with a hanky.

"Is he coming back?" Grandma asked, wrapping her arms around Frankie.

"Yeah, he's coming back," Frankie said, snuggling in her grandmother's arms. "If Blackie says he'll do something, he will."

"Then why are you crying, sweetheart?"

"'Cause I'm happy. Really happy." Frankie snuggled deeper into her grandmother's arms. "Blackie's coming home!"

All's Fine

Stop